GROVER G. GRAHAM
and Me

OTHER DELL YEARLING BOOKS YOU WILL ENJOY

JOURNEY TO NOWHERE, *Mary Jane Auch*
FROZEN SUMMER, *Mary Jane Auch*
I WAS A THIRD GRADE SCIENCE PROJECT, *Mary Jane Auch*
PRECIOUS GOLD, PRECIOUS JADE, *Sharon E. Heisel*
CHEROKEE SISTER, *Debbie Dadey*
I REMEMBER THE ALAMO, *D. Anne Love*
IN THE SHADE OF THE NÍSPERO TREE, *Carmen T. Bernier-Grand*
BE FIRST IN THE UNIVERSE, *Stephanie Spinner and Terry Bisson*
WHEN ZACHARY BEAVER CAME TO TOWN, *Kimberly Willis Holt*
IN THE QUIET, *Adrienne Ross*

DELL YEARLING BOOKS are designed especially to entertain and enlighten young people. Patricia Reilly Giff, consultant to this series, received her bachelor's degree from Marymount College and a master's degree in history from St. John's University. She holds a Professional Diploma in Reading and a Doctorate of Humane Letters from Hofstra University. She was a teacher and reading consultant for many years, and is the author of numerous books for young readers.

MARY QUATTLEBAUM

GROVER G. GRAHAM
and Me

A DELL YEARLING BOOK

Published by
Dell Yearling
an imprint of
Random House Children's Books
a division of Random House, Inc.
New York

Visit us on the Web! www.randomhouse.com/kids

Educators and librarians, for a variety of teaching tools, visit us at
www.randomhouse.com/teachers

ISBN: 0-440-41918-2

Reprinted by arrangement with Delacorte Press

Printed in the United States of America

April 2003

10 9 8 7 6 5 4

OPM

To Brad, Roland, Travis, Jack, and Spence

ACKNOWLEDGMENTS

With gratitude to the D.C. Commission on the Arts and Humanities, under the National Endowment for the Arts, for a grant in support of my creative writing during the time this book was written. A big thank-you to Sergeant Mel Quattlebaum of the Prince William County Police Department in Virginia for helpful insights into police procedures, and to Glenn Griffin, M.S.W., and Kevin Dailey, M.S.W., both with Arlington County's Family and Child Division, for their insights into the foster care system. And many, many thanks to Jennifer Wingertzahn, my editor, for her kind, careful attention to the manuscript in its various stages, and to Christopher, my husband, and Christy, my daughter, for love and good cheer throughout.

I also want to mention Brianna Blackmond, who died at the age of twenty-three months in Washington, D.C. She had been taken from a foster home and returned to the custody of her mother, and died of "blunt force trauma to the head" on January 6, 2000. Her case is under investigation. I thought of Brianna often as I worked on this novel in the months after her death.

The events of this novel take place a few months before the implementation of the Adoption and Safe Families Act of 1997.

Chapter One

This is the stupidest assignment in the history of school.

I stare down at the piece of paper on my desk. A picture of a tree. And on the tree, branches. And on the branches, twigs; and on the twigs, more twigs, tinier and tinier.

"This is your family tree," the substitute teacher said. She smiled as she passed out the papers. She acted like this assignment was special.

Special. Right. I'd rather get an F than do this.

The other kids in the class are grinning and clicking their Bics. I know they're thinking, Piece of cake. They're thinking, Patty-cake easy. Fill-in-the-blank kindergarten stuff. The other kids get right to work matching up names with twigs. Fixing each mother, father, sister, brother, aunt, uncle, cousin, grandparent, great-grandparent, and great-great-grandparent to just the right spot.

I write three names on my tree.

Ben Watson.

Sarah Jewel Watson.

Nadine Watson.

Me. My mother. My great-grandmother, Gram.

This is pitiful. There should be more names but I don't know them. I don't know the name of my father. I don't know the name of my grandmother, who is the twig between my mother and Gram. And there's no one to ask. Nadine Watson is dead. Sarah Jewel Watson is gone who knows where.

I'm a foster kid. Ben Watson, child of the system. I could write "Division of Family and Child Services" on one of my twigs. I guess I belong to them. But the system is not exactly what you would call "family." It's an office in Greenfield County, Virginia. It pays real families to take in kids who don't have one.

I think of all the foster families I've been with. I don't belong on their trees; I don't want them on mine.

I stare out the window at some real trees: sweetgums drooping at the edge of the school. It's October and their seed balls, all thorny, have changed from green to brown. I watch one plop to the ground. Folks in books are always praising the mighty oak and pretty maple, but no one says a good word about sweetgums. That's because they are pests, pure and simple. The only thing sweet is the name. This time of year, their prickly gumballs litter the earth. Kids kick them, cars squash them, grownups rake and burn them. And still they manage to take root and grow. I guess they don't know they're not wanted.

I hear other pens scratching. I make mine scratch, too. I'm coloring in my tree, a deep inky blue. The substitute teacher is giving us one whole week to complete this assignment—the stupidest in the history of school—so I may as well make it last.

I run my thumb over the names on my tree. Three names, that's enough family for me. But this past summer, for a while, I felt I had more. A brother. A crying, creeping, get-into-everything brother. A grimy, grinning gumball of a kid.

Grover G. Graham.

I write his name beside mine on my tree. Then I cross it out. That kid and I don't belong together. We don't share one single twig. I make a big ink block over his name. A blank.

But still I know the name is there, underneath. Just like I know the real Grover was with me.

I continue inking the trunk of my tree. The summer comes back to me: June, July, August. Especially August. And what I did. Did I help Grover or make his life harder? My social worker, the police—everyone has an opinion.

Me, I'm not sure anymore.

I want to think through what happened. That hot June day, the day I met Grover, seems the best place to start. I remember I was headed to my eighth foster home.

Chapter Two

Bounce-bounce-bounce. With each bump of the car, the beads in Ms. Burkell's cornrows bounced. Red-green-blue. Bounce-bounce-bounce. Cheery as bells on a Christmas reindeer.

Except this was June. And Ms. Burkell, my social worker, was frowning.

"Ben," she said, "I'm sorry things didn't work out with the Hartmans."

I shrugged. Moving happens in the system. I know kids who've been with fifteen, sixteen families, with group homes in between. Here I was headed for Number Eight.

"I think you'll like the Torgles," she went on.

Torgle. Sounded like a troll, squatty and dumb.

"They have three kids with them now. You'll have lots of company."

I didn't want company.

"This is just for a few weeks, you know. We'll work on finding you something more permanent."

Permanent. Right. The only thing permanent about the system is that nothing is permanent.

"Let's see, what else can I tell you?" Ms. Burkell tugged at a bead. "The Torgles are in their late fifties and used to young kids. But I told them you were not mouthy, not difficult. I said, 'Not Ben. No. You'll hardly know he's around.' I said . . ."

Ms. Burkell's words went on and on and *on*. So the Torgle trolls didn't want me, huh? I was used to that. Leave me alone, that's all I ask.

"Just for the summer. At most," Ms. Burkell finished up. Bounce-bounce-bounce. She sighed. "Ben, sometimes I wonder what you're thinking."

"Nothing," I said, staring out the window at the brown grass by the highway. Greenfield—right. Whoever named this county must have been as stupid and cheery as Ms. Burkell's beads. Dirtville—that's more like it. The most boring county in the state of Virginia. A place people left as soon as they could. Hadn't the Hartmans given Greenfield the boot as soon as they found decent jobs? They'd given me their new address in North Carolina so I could keep in touch.

Keep in touch. Right. No one bothered to keep in touch with me, so why should I be the first?

"I think we're almost there." Ms. Burkell squinted at a faded sign.

Jeesh, this was the sticks. Grass, trees, grass, trees, and once in a while—whoa, big excitement—a dingy farmhouse. At least the Hartmans had lived in town, close to the library, to Safeway, to Greenfield's lame idea of civilization. Too bad school was out for the summer. Sixth grade had been boring, but it was Disneyland compared to this.

I eyeballed the long stretch of heat-shimmered highway. Let my mind go blank. Before moving to a new family, I always tried to clear my mind of what happened before, sharpen up for what was to come. That's a trick I learned young. Let your mind go empty—blank as white paper— and see what happens to fill it. If a face came up, I pushed it out quick. No sense dwelling on families I'd lived with. But sometimes it took longer to push some folks out. I'd have to work on my blanking technique.

Updike. Blank. Crawdich. Blank. O'Donald. Blank. Englesham. DeBernard. Shaw. Hartman. Blank. Blank. Blank. Blank. Seven foster families. Seven blanks. And my parents, probably the biggest blanks of all. I mean, my father was a blank to the entire county. To hear Gram tell it, my mother, Sarah Jewel Watson, boarded a Greyhound bus two days after graduating high school. She returned seven months later. Returned with a baby big in her belly.

I was that baby. She left again not long after I was born.

When I lived with Gram, I never gave my mother much thought. I had never known her, so what could I miss? Gram said Sarah Jewel had inherited the footloose gene from the Watson side of the family. Some families pass on blue eyes or curly hair; the Watsons passed on feet always wanting to leave.

No one could call Gram footloose. After all, she was a Watson only by marriage. Gram had stayed stuck in Greenfield like a stubborn old pine, with roots deep in the soil.

Only her mind had roamed. It never traveled to real places, though, like Wyoming or New York City. It headed for the past. With no suitcase and no ticket to mess with, Gram's mind could be gone in a flash. I'd be sitting with her at the kitchen table, she'd stare at the checked curtains and—*poof!*—she'd be off visiting folks she knew a long time ago. And dropping names I'd never heard of. Gram could go on and on and *on*. I'd just fool with the salt and pepper shakers and wait for her mind to come back.

And when it did, Gram would give a slow, surprised blink, then smile and murmur, "Ben." I'd carefully line up the shakers—they were shaped like horses—and smile back. It was a relief to hear my name. I worried sometimes she might forget who I was. Or get stuck forever in the past.

After her mind trips, Gram would always fix us a snack. She'd rub some Ben-gay into her knobby hands—to get them working right—and slowly, slowly untwist the lid on the Jif jar. "Time for a little pick-me-up," she'd say, smoothing peanut butter on a cracker for me. Sometimes her arthritis was so bad the cracker trembled and broke. She'd just stick it back together with Jif.

Jif, extra crunchy, was our favorite food—even if it gummed up Gram's false teeth. "I'll just clean them extra good," she'd mumble, then gently tap my head. "Ben, do you know why my teeth are like the stars?"

I knew the answer—Gram asked the question at least once a day—but I'd always respond, "Why?"

She'd grin her perfect-teeth grin. "Because they come out at night."

It wasn't a very good joke—Gram wasn't much good at jokes—but I liked the mind-picture it made. I liked imagining the stars above shining bright at the very moment Gram tucked her dentures into their cup. I liked knowing those stars were up in the sky, like Gram was right there, in the next room, snoring her old-lady snore.

I lived with Gram until she died. Six years ago. I was five then. Although I have never tried to blank her out, somehow she is disappearing. I can't remember the exact color of her eyes. Her hair is a blur. I've tried sneaking up on a mirror, hoping to catch a glimpse of Gram in my face. No luck. I see only me. Brown eyes, brown hair, a blend-in kind of face. I'm like a camouflage fish I once saw on TV. It could go freckled like sand while on the ocean floor or go brown while floating near rock. You couldn't tell it was there.

Not that I'm complaining. Blend in—that's my advice to any kid in the system. Don't be too loudmouth tough or too sweet-soft. Don't be too smart or too stupid. Don't do drugs; you'll get so needy-greedy you're sure to be squashed. Keep cash in a safe place. Keep secrets to yourself. Keep holding on to that mind-picture of you at eighteen, leaving the system, walking away from it all.

Yeah, walking away from it all. Walking away from this place. Running . . . racing . . . *rocketing*. Leaving everything and everyone behind. I guess I inherited that Watson footloose gene after all.

"Ben, do you want to listen to the radio?" Ms. Burkell reached for the knob but I shook my head no.

I kept my face to the car window so she couldn't guess my thoughts. We passed a few sweetgum trees, limp in the heat. Of the families I'd lived with, two had moved on. Number Five and Number Seven. The DeBernards and Myron, their dog, were sunbathing in Florida. The Hartmans were setting off tomorrow for North Carolina.

Blank. Blank. Actually, the Hartmans, my Number Seven, weren't so bad. They were young. They liked me to call them Kitty and Ken. At their house I'd had my own room, plus an old TV and computer.

But I never saw such a couple for kissing. Smooch-smooch in the kitchen. Smooch-smooch in the living room. I never knew where I'd find them. I guess they were practicing parent stuff on me until they made a kid of their own.

All that kissing was embarrassing, so I spent a lot of time in my room. I kept a jar of Jif there and a box of saltines, for any times I got hungry. When the two Ks didn't get home till late, I'd make me a peanut butter supper, read a book, watch some TV. Maybe I'd mosey into town.

My feet always made tracks for the library and Safeway. Their air-conditioning was the best in Greenfield. And I liked their long rows of careful shelves where each thing—each book or carton or can—had its own place. Not to mention the discount tables! You could buy stuff cheap off those tables. Smashed cupcakes and spotted bananas at Safeway. Old magazines and books at the library.

The library discount table always held a big stack of *National Geographic*s. I loved turning the pages, studying the photos of oceans and deserts. I loved the names of far-off places: the Amazon, Mozambique, Zaire. I'd imagine setting off with my suitcase, going wherever I wanted. Wyoming, maybe. That state had miles of mountains and fields. Or New York City, with thousands of buildings jutting clear to the sky. What did Greenfield County have? Faded houses. Scrubby grass. Sweetgum trees.

No wonder the Hartmans decided to leave. And of course, they didn't want to take a foster kid with them.

"Keep in touch." Kitty had pressed the scrap of yellow paper—their new address—on me before Ms. Burkell drove up. Ken tried to shake my hand.

The road to the Torgles' wasn't long enough for a good blanking out. I barely had time to say "Good-bye, Number Seven. Hello, Number Eight" before the car had jerked off the highway, wound round some snake-skinny road, then hit a dirt driveway so rutty it set Ms. Burkell's beads to jumping like frogs.

"Here we are." Ms. Burkell nodded at a house as dingy as all the others we'd passed. The front porch sagged. I saw a busted lawn chair, a rickety stroller, a bike with only one wheel. And a sweetgum, of course.

Number Eight. Home sweet home.

Chapter Three

Ms. Burkell stepped out her door. "Mmmm, that fresh air." She clutched her notebook, smoothed down her skirt.

I stepped out, too, trying not to hear the *ta-dum* of my heart. Number Eight. I held tight to the blanked-out space in my mind.

Ms. Burkell continued to chatter about that air. She was trying hard—too hard—to get me excited. Ms. Burkell was always trying too hard. New to the system, you could tell.

Social workers. The ones who tried too hard weren't much better than the ones who barely remembered to call. Ms. Burkell was my fifth. She was full of shrink questions: "How do you *feel?*" She was into eye contact and Ben-ing. "Ben, do you . . ." or "Ben, look at . . ." Maybe Ms. Burkell constantly used my name to make sure she didn't forget it.

It would be an easy name to forget. Ben Watson. A blend-in kind of name.

While Ms. Burkell sniffed and smiled, I checked out the Torgles' place. Their sweetgum looked pretty scrawny, just a mess of dusty leaves. At Number Two, the Crawdiches' tree loomed twenty times larger, with gumballs big as my fist.

Mrs. Crawdich liked to show me the five-pointed leaves and explain their changing color. A tree usually turns just one shade in the fall, she told me. But a sweetgum can surprise you. She had once seen a tree with amazing leaves all yellow, dark purple, and red. It was, she said, like a bouquet of stars.

That would be something to see.

Of course we never had these talks if Mr. Crawdich was home. Then we both kept quiet, kept still. He worked hard, Mrs. Crawdich explained, smoothing my hair. He hated to be disturbed.

And I sure disturbed him. I'd drop my fork or swing my legs or make some noise with my nose and—*bam!*— Mr. Crawdich would throw down his newspaper, yell, "Can't a man have some peace?" and march me to the hall closet for time-out.

After about a million time-outs, Mr. Crawdich complained to the system. I was too difficult, he said. When my social worker took me away, Mrs. Crawdich stood very still at the window. I waved till she was out of sight. I was six then. I wouldn't do that now.

Number Eight. My eyes moved past the puny sweetgum to the bike, dented and rusty. Pitiful. The Torgle trolls must be desperate for the system's monthly check.

This place was *quiet*. That part I did like.

Then the house erupted. One, two—six?—little girls blurred through the door, followed by a slobbery mutt and a tiny woman with a face as saggy as her house. Around the corner lumbered a man, big as Frankenstein. As red faced as the woman was wrinkled. The opposite of squatty.

All of them, coming for me.

I wanted to hide—but where? I put on my blankest face.

Ms. Burkell stepped forward, her hand extended.

The woman leaped, quick as a flea, to take it.

Suddenly my own hand was grabbed by a huge red one. "Ahhh," said the man, pumping hard.

"Ahhh"? What was that supposed to mean? The man even talked like a monster.

A shriek blasted from inside the house.

The man smiled. "Sounds like the baby is up from his nap."

I snatched back my hand. I swear it was numb. A *baby*? What a pain. Number Seven was fading fast. Good-bye, peace and quiet. Good-bye, books and computer games and hours alone. Good-bye, kissy Kitty and Ken.

Hello . . . who knew what?

Every kid in the system has a dream about leaving it. Getting a place of his own. Staying as long as he wants. Deciding for himself when it's time to move on.

As the Torgles smiled and stared I tried to blank out the moment. I blanked out the moment and filled up on the dream.

Chapter Four

Turned out the six little girls were really just two. Identical twins. Kate and Jango Wells, some distant kin to Mrs. Torgle. Blood, then (though barely), not foster.

They buzzed around my suitcase like wasps.

"We're seven, but I'm ninety-four minutes older."

"My real name is Lenora but Daddy calls me Jango. You know why? Because of my voice. Daddy says I sound sweet. As jingo-jango sweet as a tinkly bell."

Tinkly bell—ha. The kid was shrill as an alarm clock.

"DADDY CALLS ME KATE THE GREAT."

And the other could scream like a siren.

"Quiet, please." The woman might be small as a flea, but her voice was far from tiny. "We don't want to overwhelm our new guest."

Guest. Right.

That banshee screech came from the house again. Mr. Torgle lurched inside.

"Well, Ben," Ms. Burkell said, "I'll leave you now, in

14

good hands. You've got my phone number? And the Hart-mans' new address?"

I thought of the yellow scrap of paper. Balled up. At the bottom of the trash can in my old room.

Blank. The paper was gone.

Ms. Burkell Ben-ed me a few times, reaching out to touch my shoulder. I stepped back. Maybe her other strays got huggy. Not me.

"I'll call soon." Ms. Burkell climbed into her car and—*poof!*—disappeared into the driveway dust.

I could hardly wait for the day I left that easy. I'd roar off in something fine and fast. A motorcycle, maybe. No bone-shaking heap of metal for me.

When I looked back, the twins had fixed their eyes on me. Each held tight to a Barbie doll dressed in a ratty sock. Two pairs of big blue kid eyes. Two pairs of big blue Barbie eyes. One girl stuck the foot of her doll in her mouth and sucked it like a thumb.

This had to be my strangest foster home yet.

"We're here temporary," said Kate (or maybe Jango).

"Our daddy's going to take us back soon. He's looking for a job in South Carolina."

Right. Like I hadn't heard that before. Don't all strays want some parent, like a fairy godmother, to swoop out of nowhere and whisk them away?

I got rid of that wish a long time ago.

"You don't have nobody," the Barbie-chewing twin told me. "That's what Mrs. T. said."

Yeah, kid, I thought. But at least I have a real nobody—and not a daddy who's just a dream.

"Kate, Jango." Mrs. Torgle's voice took on a no-

nonsense tone. "Let's help Ben with his things." She reached for my suitcase.

I folded my fist over the handle. "I take my own gear," I said.

Mrs. Torgle slowly withdrew her hand. The dog stopped wagging her tail.

I take my own gear. I'd learned to do that at Saint Stephen's Juvenile Home. I'd been dumped there while my social worker hunted up a new placement, after Number Four gave me the boot. One of those Saint Stephen's boys—oh, he had a big, shiny smile. He oozed helpfulness. Showed me around the group home. But that night, going to sleep, I realized ten dollars had vanished from my pocket. Bright smile, light fingers.

The dog wiggled her big head up under my hand.

"Charmaine likes to sleep on the rug in Jake's room," said one twin. "She gets lonely."

Great. Exactly what I wanted—a mutt so needy she'd welcome any old pat.

Charmaine rolled a long tongue over my hand and panted. Jeesh, did she need a toothbrush! I remembered the dog at Number Five, the DeBernards. Myron the Chihuahua had a toothbrush. He also had three sweaters, a plaid jacket, and a yellow rain visor to protect his pop eyes. Myron didn't like to be patted. Whenever I had tried, he bared his clean white teeth.

A gob of Charmaine slobber hit my shoe. Yuck. Give me Myron any day.

Before I could wipe it off, Mr. Torgle monster-stepped out of the house, carrying a yellow-haired baby.

"Grover." One twin rolled her eyes. "Grover G. Graham."

"He's more than a year old and he *still* cries constantly."

"And he *pees* in his diaper."

"His mother comes over sometimes. She—"

"Girls!" Mrs. Torgle interrupted. "Let's show Ben to his room."

I gripped my suitcase and followed her to the house.

Walking backward, facing me, one twin said, "Grover drools worse than Charmaine."

Grover opened his mouth for another wail. Pat-pat-pat. Mr. Torgle's hand covered the baby's whole back. Pat-pat-pat. The kid's open mouth turned into a watery smile. He flapped his fat fist.

"That means good-bye . . . or maybe hello," the other twin explained.

Suddenly—*whonk!*—Charmaine's tail slammed my knee with the force of a truck.

I gritted my teeth. I'd like to flap my fist and say a few good-byes. It was a good thing I had blanked out Kitty and Ken. Otherwise, I'd be starting to miss them.

Mrs. Torgle opened the porch door, with its broken screen. "I'm going to fix that soon," Mr. Torgle said to her. "Better sooner than later," she threw back, darting into the house. What a weird couple, I thought, trying to keep up. Flea and Frankenstein. Personally I'd rather have trolls.

We passed through the living room: brown furniture, brown carpet, tan walls. Your basic no-stain, no-pain colors. Pictures cluttered every square inch. I thought of the pictures at Gram's. A few photos of Sarah Jewel, the girl she called my mother. Long, dark hair is all I recall.

Even moving double-quick through the Torgles' living room, I noticed it was practically a shrine. Picture after picture after picture of the same person at different ages. Enough to make you dizzy. Big smile, blond hair, big smile, blond hair—all framed in silver or gold.

Their real kid, I bet.

The Torgles probably take in strays now 'cause they're missing their own, I thought, clumping my suitcase up the stairs. Two old folks hungry for a pat. Just like their dog.

Mrs. Torgle waved me through a door. "We'll let you get settled in your room."

I turned to the bureau—and discovered "we" hadn't left. The twins started jiggling one of my suitcase locks.

"Don't," I commanded. The jiggling continued.

My room. Right.

"We're *welcoming* you." One girl pointed to a row of trophies above the bureau. "Those are Jake's."

Of course Jake would be a jock.

"He's in South America now," said the other. "He teaches in a home for orphans."

A saint, too. Another Ms. Burkell nosing into the lives of strays.

"Look!" The girls giggled, waving their Barbies. "Charmaine is *tasting* your suitcase."

The dog's tongue rolled over the brown vinyl. Yuck. I grabbed her collar and pushed her into the hall.

"Out," I commanded the girls, who left, still laughing.

I closed the bedroom door. Privacy—finally. With the bottom of my T-shirt, I wiped the dog drool off my suitcase. It had been a good-bye gift from Myron, according to the DeBernards, who were always putting words into the dog's mouth. "Myron says bye-bye, Ben," Mrs.

DeBernard had trilled, waving the Chihuahua's paw when I was leaving. Myron had gazed at me with his serious eyes and for once let me scratch his ears.

When I blank out Number Five, I try not to include Myron. I like remembering the smooth, warm hair on his small, bony head.

I opened the suitcase, stuck my clothes in the drawers, and buried my Jif and saltines under my shirts. Then I fingered the tiny locks I'd added to the suitcase's six zippered pockets. All my money nestled safe inside the second pocket: $129.37. I personally knew every dollar, quarter, and dime. The sweat of my brow turned into cash. Walking Myron and scooping his poop. Hoarding change doled out for my school lunch. Doing a thousand chores for all my foster families.

I wondered how much money Sarah Jewel Watson took when she left Greenfield.

I unlocked the fifth pocket and drew out a tissue-wrapped bundle. Carefully I removed each layer, ran my thumb over the plastic tip, then plugged it into the outlet.

Instantly a soft blue glow.

My night-light. Mrs. Crawdich, at Number Two, had given it to me a long time ago, after a spell of bad dreams. She was afraid my crying would wake up her husband. And so was I. I didn't want to be marched to the time-out closet at midnight.

Luckily the night-light had worked.

So I've kept it with me. I don't need it now, not like when I was a little kid, but the blue glow feels nice in a strange room. It helps ease the first night in a new place.

Stretching out on Number Eight's too soft bed, I focused on the blue light, then slowly closed my eyes. I always prepared carefully for the first night in a new foster home. I didn't want those dreams sneaking back in. I blanked out the feel of Number Seven's bed. In my mind, I tried to see Number Eight's brown-plaid bedspread and row of gold trophies.

A soft creak. The door?

Those nosey twins. "Out," I said, not opening my eyes.

There was no sound of a door closing. Instead came *swish, swish, swish.*

Now I was mad. My blank-out time was completely shot.

"What part of 'out' don't you understand?" I snarled, jumping up.

I was in time to see that little blond kid toddling straight for my night-light.

"No!" I shouted.

He stopped. Turned. Opened his mouth.

"Waaaahh!"

"Oh, jeesh, baby." I didn't move. "Don't cry."

"Waaaahhh!"

I leaned over and peered into his face. "Baby, where are the tears? I bet you're faking."

"Waaaahhhhh!"

What do I do with a screaming kid? Should I call Mrs. Torgle? I'd never dealt with a baby. The only thing close had been Myron the Chihuahua, and he never made this kind of noise.

I reached down and sort of palmed the baby's head. He bawled louder.

So I picked him up and looked him straight in the face.

"Baby," I said. "Shut up."

Then I brought him closer and went pat-pat-pat to his back. The way Mr. Torgle had patted. Pat-pat-pat.

And just like that, he shut up.

So I patted some more, feeling dumb. How did you know you were doing it right? And when could you stop? This patting could go on forever.

But soon the kid started squirming and I set him down. He flapped his fist, then—*swish, swish, swish*—toddled out.

I shut the door tight and shook my head at the gold trophy men. "Please," I said, "let me leave soon."

Chapter Five

My first week at the Torgles': chaos with a capital *C*. Even school was better than this. Ms. Burkell needed to come up with Number Nine—fast. These little kids were driving me nuts.

Kate and Jango were two motormouths that constantly revved.

And Grover G. Graham was the exact opposite of his prissy bow tie of a name. Grover was a cross between a bulldozer and a vacuum. He was constantly pounding, tearing, bashing. Constantly slurping everything into his mouth. My ears got to be better than Charmaine's. Hyper-alert for that *swish, swish, swish*. The sound of his busy legs moving inside his diaper. I knew, then, that he was nearby. Destroying all in his path.

I should know. My first night at Number Eight, Flea and Frankenstein told me that all us kids were expected to help out around the house. One of my "chores" would be to watch the little destroyer for an hour or so each day while

Mrs. Torgle cleaned up the house or washed clothes. At fourteen months, Grover might be just a bit larger than a Chihuahua, but he was a thousand times more trouble. Myron never tried to lick dirt. He never screeched or kicked. He walked politely on his leash. Myron loved to snooze, too, unlike Grover, who, I swear, wanted to play peekaboo for hours. And who cried whenever I stopped.

As if watching Grover weren't "chore" enough, I also had to sweep floors and clean the porch and wash the rattletrap car—all for the grand sum of zero. I was a guy Cinderella. My suitcase pocket would be stuck at $129.37 until some Number Nine took me in.

My first Friday there Frankenstein asked if I could watch the kids by myself for an hour. He needed to take Mrs. T. to the dentist and pick up his check from the hardware store where he worked.

I shrugged. Basically I avoided Mr. T. The girls might scramble all over him, but the way he lurched and aahed gave me the creeps. I figured an hour was only sixty minutes. How much trouble could two little girls, one dog, and one baby make in that time?

Believe me, they can make a lot.

Kate started as soon as the Torglemobile rattled down the drive. It had taken me a week to figure how to tell the twins apart. Kate was taller and bossier. Jango sucked her Barbie's feet.

In her typical bossy style, Kate announced she was going to make popcorn.

I shook my head. "No one eats popcorn right after breakfast."

"I do." Kate measured oil into a big pan, then threw in two handfuls of kernels.

I thought about Ms. Burkell's words. The Torgles liked little kids because they were less difficult. Ha!

"Kate—"

"Mrs. T. would let me," Kate said, fiddling with the knobs on the stove.

"No, she wouldn't." I grabbed the pan and turned off the stove.

"My daddy would."

"He's not around."

Kate burst into tears.

I rolled my eyes. Why the big boo-hoo? I was just telling it like it was.

Then Jango screamed from upstairs: "Ben, it's *Grover*!"

Was the baby choking? Bleeding? I raced through the living room, dumped the pan on top of the TV, then took the stairs two at a time.

I burst into Jake's room to find Jango hollering and Charmaine barking. Grover was scratching at my night-light. He tugged it from the outlet.

"No!" I yelled.

The kid took one look at me. Blinked.

And popped the night-light into his mouth.

In two strides I had him. My finger poked into his mouth and scooped out the night-light.

His baby teeth came down hard.

"Ow!" I yelled.

"Thank *God*." Jango flopped dramatically across the bed. "I thought Grover was going to fry."

I wiped the night-light on my T-shirt while Grover

blinked up at me. He looked innocent as Tweety Bird. What if he *had* stuck his finger in the outlet? Or broken the night-light and cut himself? Or swallowed a piece of plastic?

Suddenly my legs felt shaky. "Jango," I scolded, "you should have been watching—"

"Me?" Jango bounced up. "You're the *baby*-sitter."

Suddenly the TV blared. *BLEEEEP*. Kate was into something, for sure. I hoisted Grover on my hip and hauled him downstairs. Jango followed. With every step she jabbed the pointy feet of her Barbie into my back.

Kate was hunched about two inches from the screen, watching a woman shake her fist at a fat man. The TV bleeped every two seconds. Bleeping out cusswords.

"KATE!" I yelled. Jango's Barbie stabbed my rib. "TURN IT DOWN."

Her eyes remained on the screen. "You didn't say please."

Say please? To a bossy seven-year-old brat?

I grabbed for the volume knob on the TV. Grover grabbed for the pan on top.

One of us succeeded.

The pan flipped in the air.

Everything happened in slow motion then, like in the movies. The pan sailed end over end . . . kernels sprayed . . . drops of oil shimmered and plopped. I felt my leg rise . . . my hand open and reach. . . .

Thud. The pan landed, bottom side up, on the carpet.

"Oops," said Kate.

"It wasn't me," declared Jango.

BLEEP, screamed the TV. *BLEEEEEP*.

Grover's pudgy hands came together. Clap-clap-clap.

Oil dripped down the TV screen, where the woman was now choking the man. I'd like to get Kate in my own stranglehold, I thought, picking up the pan.

"Oops," Kate said again.

Underneath the pan was a picture of Saint Jake Jock. Once the guy had smiled from a gold frame on top of the TV. Now oil oozed across his face. Kernels speckled it like zits.

"Ahhh."

I froze—but Grover didn't. I could feel him squirm in my arms.

Mr. T. loomed in the doorway. His big, square head turned left, then right. His hand reached out.

Snap went the TV knob. The screaming couple vanished.

I tightened my hold on Grover, who gurgled and grabbed my nose. I watched Mr. T.'s hand return to his side. What would our punishment be?

Punishment. Each foster family had its own brand. Of course, you never knew what you'd get until you messed up. Some slapped, some scolded.

At Number Two, Mr. Crawdich had the time-out closet. Inside I was supposed to *think* about what I had done. Maybe I had stomped. Or clicked my toys. Or scattered gumballs in the yard. But the mothball smell in the closet made my head ache and the darkness made me sleepy. My thinking got so jumbled I had to stop. Mostly I kept my eyes on the light under the door and waited to be released.

What would Mr. Torgle do to us? I could deal with anything, I figured, but what about Grover? A little kid shouldn't be shut in a closet.

The man came at us. I watched his face. He didn't look mad, but you never could tell. At Number Five, Mrs. DeBernard could smile and scold at the very same time.

I held Grover very tight.

But I was no match for Mr. T. He lifted Grover right out of my arms.

The man hoisted that baby up, up, up. What was he going to do? "Hey, you!" Mr. T. boomed so loud that I winced.

But Grover was laughing. The kid flapped his fist like a windmill gone wild.

My legs started shaking so hard I had to sit down. Right in a pile of kernels.

"It wasn't *me*." Jango pointed her Barbie at the mess.

"Of course not." Mr. T. winked at me. "But help Ben clean up anyway."

No slapping, no scolding, no time-out closet. I felt relief wash over me. Maybe Frankenstein wasn't so creepy after all.

Kate flopped on the rug beside me. "Clean up now?" she whined. "I'm tired."

"Well, you know what Mrs. T. says." The man carried Grover into the kitchen. "Better sooner than later."

I'd gotten my legs under control by then and started picking up kernels. Kate and Jango swiped at the carpet with paper towels. I could hear Mr. T. aahing at Grover in the next room. For once that monster sound didn't grate on my nerves.

"My daddy wouldn't make me do this," Kate grumbled, smearing the oil on the TV screen.

Your daddy's not around, I wanted to say again—but didn't. I remembered her tears. Kate was learning fast enough that "Daddy" was just a dream. No sense rubbing it in.

Chapter Six

The next week was as chaotic as the first. If Ms. Burkell didn't call soon, I'd hunt up my own Number Nine.

My second Friday there, I was taking a well-deserved break in Jake's room, thinking about my plans. I crunched a peanut butter cracker. Mrs. T.'s meals were okay—meat, mashed potatoes, red Jell-O—but I liked having my Jif close by. It gave me the same safe feeling as knowing $129.37 nestled snug in my suitcase and my blue light was tucked in the wall. The same feeling as having my plans stashed in my mind.

I caught crumbs carefully in my palm. Wouldn't want to mess up Jake's spread. Wouldn't want the Torgles complaining to Ms. Burkell that the new kid was being difficult. I crunched again and, in my mind, began to lay out my plans. Even though I've laid them out a hundred—a thousand—times before, it is pure pleasure to get them lined up again, all in a row, neat as Saint Jake Jock's trophies.

I've got goals. Most kids in the system have got nothing but dreams. When they grow up—oh, wow!—they're going to be a rock star or a rich lawyer or a model. Right. They got no plan to go from A to Z.

Me, I don't jet through the alphabet. I go A, B, C.

A. Start with "now." I'm eleven years old.

B. At eighteen I graduate and leave school, leave the system, leave Greenfield County forever.

C. I get a job somewhere nice, maybe Safeway. There are Safeways all over the country. I could go to Wyoming. Or maybe New York City.

A, B, C. That's how my life was laid out.

Bang! went the door and—wouldn't you know—the twins barged in.

"Ben," said one.

"Guess who's coming?" said the other.

I didn't even open my mouth. I knew they'd soon answer their own question.

And they did.

"Tracey," they cried together. "Grover's mom."

"Her purse is full of the coolest stuff." Jango plopped beside me on the bed. "About fourteen lipsticks and black stuff for your eyes."

"How do you know?"

"Kate looked. Mrs. T. made her apologize."

I rolled my eyes. "Your snooping is going to get you in *big* trouble someday."

"Your snooping is going to get you in *big* trouble someday," Kate mimicked. She sniffed hugely, like

Charmaine. "Peanut butter," she pronounced. "Are you eating in here? You'll attract ants, you know. That's what Mrs. T. says."

I let her go on and on, knowing she'd soon find another topic.

"Tracey had Grover when she was fifteen or something."

Here was the new topic.

"Ben, how old are you?"

"Older than you."

"He's eleven," chimed in Jango. "I heard Mrs. T. say."

Kate gave me this *look*. "So in four years you could have a baby."

I snorted. "Don't plan on it."

"That would make us aunts." Jango nibbled her Barbie's foot.

"No, it wouldn't," I said. "You have to be related."

"Well, we could be *pretend* aunts," Kate said.

"Listen, you guys. You can't be aunts, pretend or otherwise." I spoke very slowly so these two ditzes would get it. "There . . . will . . . be . . . no . . . *baby*."

Jango giggled.

"But we're aunts to Grover," said Kate. "Mrs. T. said we could be. You can be his uncle."

"No thanks." The twins weren't going to drag me into any make-believe family. I knew how that went. Kissy-kissy, huggy-huggy—but when foster Mommy and Daddy moved or found you "difficult" or had kids of their own, believe me, you were out the door. I remembered Mrs. Crawdich standing sadly at the window when I left—and quickly blanked her out. It was better to stay free of mush. It wouldn't be long before Saint Jake Jock had a family of his own. Once they had grandkids, the Torgles wouldn't want strays.

Just then we heard the *bumpety-bump* of a car in the rutty drive, and Kate and Jango barged out the door. I stayed upstairs. Quiet in that house was so rare I wanted to enjoy it. Even Charmaine and her knee-cracking tail had disappeared.

I made another peanut butter cracker but couldn't get my mind back on my list. Maybe the house was *too* quiet. I better go see what those two snoops were into.

As I tromped down the stairs and passed the living room—that shrine to Saint Jake Jock—I caught a glimpse of Grover. The little guy was sitting up, proud as could be, patting a skinny tin case. "Ga-ba-da. Ga-*ba*-da."

The girl with him had long, frizzy hair and some black goop on her lashes. This was Tracey? She didn't look much like a mother to me.

"Do you like your present, Grover?" the girl asked.

The kid was scratching, scratching. At a scrawny brush and five dabs of paint.

Was this girl stupid or what? Grover, the human vacuum cleaner, would suck that stuff—*shloop*—straight into his mouth.

Sure enough, out flicked his little red tongue.

"No, Grover," said the girl.

He lifted the case to his mouth.

"No."

No wasn't going to stop Grover. I remembered him blinking at me when I had yelled the word. Then popping my night-light into his mouth.

"No." The girl removed the paint case from the pudgy fist.

Of course, Grover howled.

I knew I shouldn't get involved—this was his mother—but that "waaah" sounded pitiful.

"Hide the paints," I suggested. "Give him a toy to play with."

The girl flashed a look at me. Like I was calling her stupid or something. Then her eyes hardened.

"Everyone tries to tell me how to take care of my kid," she said. "He has to learn the meaning of 'no.' "

Grover continued to cry.

Poor little guy. I waited for the girl to do something, but she didn't move. So I reached down and picked the kid up. Pat-pat-patted his back. Grover sniffled once and rubbed his face on my shirt. Tears and drool all over.

That fast, the girl grabbed the baby.

I stumbled back. "Hey! I was just trying to help."

"I know what to do."

Grover whimpered and reached for me.

The girl's face turned red. "You an expert?" she sneered at me, jiggling Grover in a way I knew he hated. "You been raised by a perfect mama?"

Her words stung. What did she know about me or Sarah Jewel? As for "expert," I probably knew her kid better than she did. Where was she when I was taking care of him every day?

I looked the girl up . . . down, from the spider-lash eyes to the tight T-shirt to the red stuff on her toenails. "My mama's probably about as perfect as you," I said coldly, walking out the door.

Back in Jake's room I sat on the bed. I tried to blank out the paint set. I tried to blank out the girl.

But there are some things you can't blank out. What if Grover had choked on that teeny brush? Or poisoned himself with the paints?

I gazed up at Jake's gold trophy men. It's not fair, I thought. Some kids get born to two parents, their own rooms, refrigerators stuffed with hot dogs and Twinkies.

And other kids get a mother like Tracey.

I bet Sarah Jewel was like Tracey. If so, I'm glad she disappeared. I'd rather be alone than with a mother like that. I can take care of myself.

But Grover was a baby. Who'd take care of him?

I marched back downstairs, straight to the kitchen, where Mrs. T. was cracking eggs in a bowl.

I said, "Shouldn't you be supervising?"

Mrs. Torgle's wrinkles folded up in surprise.

No wonder. Up to this point, our conversations had consisted of her asking whether I wanted more potatoes or Jell-O and me answering yes or no.

"What do you mean?" she asked.

Well, if there's one thing the system teaches, it's not to squeal. Do you think you'd last long running to foster Mommy with tales about another kid? No. Keep your mouth shut, stay out of the way. That's the best way to deal.

But here I was, steering dead straight for trouble.

I crossed my arms. "You should be in the living room with Grover."

Mrs. Torgle put down her spoon. "What's wrong?"

So I told her. I squealed like a piggy going to market.

Wee-wee-wee. All about the paint set and the stupid mother and the crying baby.

Mrs. Torgle sighed. "Poor Tracey."

Poor *Tracey?* What about Grover?

"Tracey had a hard go of it when her parents died. But she's learning how to take care of her baby. There's a special class—"

"Well, she's flunking."

Mrs. Torgle's wrinkles settled into a frown. "Don't be too hard on her, Ben—"

"What did Tracey do," I interrupted, "that made her lose Grover?"

"She didn't *lose* him." A sharp tone edged her words. "This is a temporary arrangement."

Believe me, I know the system. A mother's got to mess up bad to lose her baby. Even temporarily. I know kids with more bruises than a stomped-on banana. A gift from home sweet home.

"Grover seems fine now." Mrs. Torgle listened to the quiet murmurs from the living room. "Would you like to lick the cake bowl?"

It took a moment for her words to sink in. Would I like to lick the cake bowl? Give me a break. I was looking for answers, not some little-kid treat.

I didn't bother to reply. I'd get the truth from Kate and Jango. Those two snoops were bound to know more than Mrs. T. wanted to tell.

Chapter Seven

The next day, Saturday, Mr. Torgle clapped on his cap, uttered his "ahhh," and asked if we'd like to go into town. The girls carried on like we were headed to Disneyland.

"Can we go to Uddleston's, Mr. T.?"

"They have the best milk shakes there."

I tried to blank out my own excitement. Downtown Greenfield. Big whoop. I wished we could go to the new shopping center that had just opened on Route 3. There was supposed to be a toy store there as big as a barn. I bet it was stuffed with the latest computer games. Right then, though, I'd have gone anywhere. At least visiting stores— even the ones downtown—was better than sweeping floors and watching a sweetgum grow.

As we chugged down that snake-skinny road and onto the highway, the front door beside me jiggled. "Broken lock," Mr. T. sighed.

"You'll fix it soon!" Kate yelled from the backseat.

"Better sooner than later," hollered Jango.

I had to smile. The girls had caught the Torgles perfectly: Mr. T.'s talk about fixing things—that never got fixed—and Mrs. T.'s reply.

"I guess I'm a later man." Mr. T. grinned at me while the girls giggled. "So, Ben, any place you want to go today?"

I cut my eyes at the man, surprised. Basically I was along for the ride. I never liked to ask for too much. Didn't want to be difficult.

But even though the twins squealed, "How boring!" when I answered, Mr. T. just nodded. "The library it is," he said.

Our first stop was the bank, where Mr. T. withdrew a hunk of cash from the ATM. He stuck some of the money in his wallet. The rest went into an old deposit envelope, which he tucked in the glove compartment. "If I lose my wallet," he explained to the twins, "I'll still have enough for those milk shakes."

I thought of the locks on my suitcase. Obviously Mr. T. had never met any light-fingered boys from Saint Stephen's.

Our second stop was the hardware store where Mr. T. worked. That place was such a jumble of parts and pieces and dusty stuff it's a wonder the nuts didn't think they were bolts. That new shopping center on Route 3 was supposed to have a hardware store even bigger than the toy store. I remembered seeing the picture in the newspaper when it opened. Beside it, Mr. T.'s rickety place, with its faded paint, was no better than a nail-selling shack.

But to see the man open the door, you'd think we were strolling into a palace. He said he was going to buy washers, but I knew better. He really wanted to show off the twins.

Of course, everyone oohed over their identical cuteness, mixed up their names, laughed.

I did my camouflage-fish thing, blending in. I wondered what Grover was doing back at the house. Yesterday he had noticed the gumballs on the sweetgum for the very first time. Playing under the tree's useless shade, the kid had gazed up, completely amazed. Then, murmuring, "ga-ba-da," he had reached for the prickly things hanging up there. Like he was trying to be friends.

Funny little guy.

Suddenly, in the hardware store, Mr. T. put his hand on my shoulder. "This here's Ben," he announced to nuts, bolts, and people alike. "Smart as they come. And right good with the baby."

Everyone smiled at me and nodded. I blinked back. I felt like a camouflage fish in the spotlight. Somehow, though, the spotlight seemed inside me, not outside. Kind of glowy. *Smart.* The word repeated in my head. Mr. T.'s hand on my shoulder was heavy and warm.

That glowy feeling hung on as we piled back in the car but dimmed as we drove through town. The broken lock jiggled while I gazed out the window. Everything looked so bleached by the sun that, I swear, this place should be called Fadefield. We passed the dingy cobbler's, the pharmacy and its cluttered window, the beauty salon where the haircuts all looked the same. The Hartmans' house, freshly painted not three weeks before, was the hard yellow of a yolk boiled too long. My Number Seven. I wondered if

Kitty and Ken were happy smooching in North Carolina. I blanked out a sudden sadness.

The Torglemobile kept chugging and soon was turning into a parking lot. Seven red letters gleamed on a huge store: *S-A-F-E-W-A-Y*. As its doors parted before me, I stood on the black mat for a moment, looking in. I felt the air, soundless and cool, drying the sweat on my face.

Safeway. Everything here was bright and clean. I liked rolling a wire cart up and down the ten white aisles. I liked choosing one perfect apple from a pile of fruit or comparing the prices of soup.

Shopping with Mr. T. and the twins, though, was nothing like that. Mr. T. read aloud from his list, the girls whizzed the cart, and I tossed—no, *flung*—boxes and cans into it. I bet that wire cart had never rattled so fast.

The twins chattered all the way to our next stop: Uddleston's, the ice cream shop next to the Greyhound bus station. I remembered trips there with other foster families. I always ordered a vanilla shake, thick and sweet, and tried to make it last.

As I stirred my vanilla shake I watched a Greyhound bus pull up. Sleek and silver. So full of shine it outdid the sun. I watched folks climb down the stairs, swinging their bags and cases. I watched others stepping in.

Where had they come from? Where were they going? I wondered if Sarah Jewel had watched the buses when she was a kid. If that was when her footloose gene had kicked in. I started daydreaming about the day I would be leaving. Leaving Greenfield and not looking back.

"Earth to Ben." Twin milk-shake slurps and giggles. "Come in, Ben."

Kate and Jango. Were they ever quiet? They would have *lived* in the time-out closet at the Crawdiches'.

Turning, I caught a look from Mr. T. Almost as if he could see my leaving-town dreams. I let my face go blank.

But all he said was, "Ready for the library?"

When we chugged up, car door jiggling, it was good to see the blue doors again, the space inside neat as Safeway. Almost closing time, but the twins set up such a boo-hoo for library cards that Mr. T. completed the forms right there. I spun the paperback rack, checking out covers, avoiding anything with a rose, a bird, or the color pink. Bound to be mushy. *Where Eagles Dare* showed an icy mountain, a cable car, some guy dropping to his death. I grabbed it and headed for the checkout desk, passing a row of little-kid books. *The Cat in the Hat. One Fish, Two Fish, Red Fish, Blue Fish.* The *Hop on Pop* cover showed two baby bears bouncing on a big one. Like Grover bouncing on Charmaine. Maybe the little guy would like a book. And if he didn't, at least I wouldn't be out any cash.

The librarian was looking at me, then at her watch. As I passed the used-book table one title caught my eye.

Baby and Child Care.

I picked up the book. It had a torn cover and dingy pages. It must be a hundred years old.

You an expert? I remembered Tracey Graham's sneer.

I glanced at the name of the author. Dr. Benjamin Spock. Doctor. That would make him an expert, right?

I read the back cover. The book was enlarged, revised, updated. And only twenty-five cents. Sure, it was old, but how much could babies have changed? From all I've seen on TV, the basics stay the same. Babies poop, cry, eat, mess with stuff they shouldn't. I figured I could give the book to Mrs. T. to give to Tracey. It might help more than those classes.

Chapter Eight

After dinner I headed to Jake's room with my library book, but Grover toddled after me so fast I figured, why not read together? So I settled on the living room couch with *Where Eagles Dare* and handed *Hop on Pop* to the kid.

The first thing he did? Put it in his mouth.

"Grover"—I shook my head—"that's no way to treat fine literature."

He thumped the book. "Ga-ba-da!" One of his pudgy paws hooked under a page. *Riiiip.*

"Grover, no!" I grabbed the book.

Grover reading on his own was definitely *not* working. *Hop on Pop* was checked out on my library card. Guess who'd be paying when it was trashed?

I lifted the kid and set him beside me.

"Ga," he demanded, scratching the cover.

But I took control. I held *Hop on Pop* and started to read, nice and slow. Grover kept jabbing my side, so I tucked him on my lap. He settled right down then, all cozy, with that Tweety Bird head bobbing an inch from my nose.

"Ba!" Grover pointed to a picture of two little banshees dancing on their dad. "Ba! Ba!" I could tell he was trying to say *something*, but how do you translate *ba*?

I took a stab. "Bear," I said. "One little bear. Two little bears."

"Ba!" Grover's fat little feet beat my knees.

That's how it went the entire book. I'd never taken so long to read so few words in my life. I could have read three chapters of *Where Eagles Dare* in the time it took to creep-crawl over those sixty-four pages, mixed with a million *ba*s.

When we finally reached the end, "Ba," Grover commanded, pounding the book. "Ba!"

So I read that book again. And again. Midway through the fourth reading Kate and Jango wandered through and settled beside us.

"*Please* start over," they whined. "We want to see *all* the pictures."

So I started over. After all, that bossy Kate had actually said "please"—maybe for the first time in her life.

By the time old Charmaine lumbered in, I swear, that book was engraved on my brain.

"Ba!" Grover squirmed off the couch.

"Ba!" He grabbed both Charmaine's ears.

The dog shot me this pitiful look. I figured I owed her one.

I thought that was the end of *Hop on Pop*. Jeesh, was I ever wrong. The next evening after dinner, Grover ba-ed like a demented sheep. I brought one of his chewed-on board books to the couch, but he flat-out rejected it. I'd read one sentence and the kid would be turning the page, peering under the book, crying, "Ba." It was no use. I was stuck with *Hop on Pop*.

After two more nights of this, I started to worry. Why did Grover need to hear the same story over and over? Maybe he couldn't get it fixed right in his head. Maybe he was stupid. Maybe he'd have to take special classes. The other kids would call him names. Slow Grover. Grover the Goob.

People would be mean to him.

Finally I worked myself up to asking Mrs. T. if she thought something was wrong.

She was wiping a sponge over the kitchen faucet but immediately stopped and turned. "Why?"

What could I say? I wanted to tell her—but I didn't. Grown-ups usually make a problem worse. What if she started taking Grover to doctors and shrinks? Or to a home for retarded kids?

So I fixed on the faucet, shiny and silver.

"I can tell you're worried, Ben."

I glanced at her sharply. How could she tell? I wasn't exactly a blabber. In fact, with the Torgles, I kept talk to two topics: meals and chores. Mrs. T. was tied up with the twins and Grover. I didn't need her to watch over me.

But her words showed she had been watching.

I didn't like that. I felt like a camouflage fish thrown up on the beach. Exposed. Nowhere to hide.

I made my face go blank. Fixed on the curtains above the sink. They were pea green with scrawny tassels. Gram's curtains had been checked blue and white. Like teeny squares of sky and stars.

44

The tassels drooped. Here I was, squealing again. It was getting to be a habit.

"Grover's obsessed with *Hop on Pop*," I finally got out. "He wants to hear it again and again. Something must be wrong with him."

"Oh." Mrs. T. clapped her hand to her mouth.

Horrified, I guessed.

She made a choking sound.

Laughing. The woman was laughing.

"That's just what little kids do," she finally said, wiping her eyes. "When they like something, once is never enough."

I could feel the flush move up my neck. What a fool!

"Grover is just like my Jake. Poor Mr. Torgle got stuck with *Madeline* in the very same way." Mrs. T. chuckled. "One night I caught him talking in his sleep—repeating the same words over and over." Mrs. T. droned in a deep voice like her husband's: " 'Twelve little girls in two straight lines.'

"And you know what, Ben?" Mrs. T. switched back to her regular voice. "For years Jake liked to line things up, from the peas on his plate to the pencils on his desk. Just like those little girls." She laughed again.

Well, who would have guessed? Some book called *Madeline* and Saint Jake Jock? Maybe he had even lined up his trophies. I pictured the big blond guy nudging a gold batter here, a quarterback there, getting the little guys in perfect rows.

"Well," I said with relief, "Grover's not *that* obsessed."

Mrs. T. grinned. Then she reached out and kind of rumpled my hair. I remembered Gram's tapping and Mrs. Crawdich's smoothing, but Mrs. T. had a different style.

Her fingers turned like a somersault. When she stopped, I could still feel her hand, its warm weight.

Mrs. T. returned to her cleaning. "I don't think you need to worry about Grover. He's sharp as they come. His mother—" Mrs. T. stopped short.

Grover's mother. Pouty lips. Black spider lashes. She'd canceled her visit today.

"What's wrong with Tracey?" I asked.

"She's got the flu."

I shook my head. "I mean *really* wrong."

Mrs. T. frowned slightly. She seemed to frown whenever I asked about Tracey. "She's . . . pulling herself together. She's doing her best."

Right. Her best didn't seem too good. I remembered Grover crying over that cheap present, all wrong for a baby. I remembered him reaching for me.

Mrs. T. angled the sponge at the edge of the sink, then straightened it. She said, "You think about Grover a lot, don't you, Ben?"

That question could have come straight from the mouth of my nosey social worker. Right down to the "Ben." Suddenly I was alert.

"Maybe more than you think about yourself?" asked Mrs. T.

I shrugged. Why should I think about myself? I was doing just fine, thank you very much. I carefully straightened my hair where the woman had messed with it. Mrs. T.'s shrink strategies were as obvious as Ms. Burkell's, I thought. She needed to turn her eyes in Grover's direction. That mother of his needed watching.

What had Tracey done to lose Grover, anyway? I remembered kids I'd known in the system. Banged up and bruised by their parents.

Had Tracey hurt Grover? I needed to find out, in case the kid ever needed help.

It was time for a chat with the snoops.

Chapter Nine

In two days, I saw my chance.

Grover had just gone down for a nap and I could escape. Lately the kid had taken to following me like a goat after grass. *Swish, swish, swish.* I swear that sound even entered my dreams.

Kate and Jango were playing under the sweetgum. At its best, this was one pitiful tree, but today it looked downright goofy. Christmas tinsel draped a few gumballs, and two Barbies, tied up with string, spun slowly from a branch.

And the tree wasn't the only thing dressed silly. It was sweat-sticky hot—and those girls had scarves around their necks and colored tights on their heads. "We're princesses," Kate informed me.

"You look like rabbits," I said.

Beneath the tree, Charmaine scratched at the fake holly on her collar. Red ribbons drooped from her ears.

Kate gestured proudly: "Our noble steed."

I tried to keep my eyes from rolling. I reminded myself I was doing this for Grover. "Do you want me to, uh . . . play or something?" I asked. My plan was to work in a few questions when they least suspected.

"*You* want to *play?*" Jango's eyes opened wide. "With *us?*"

Maybe this wasn't such a good idea.

"You've got to play right, Ben," Kate said, "or you're out. What do you want to be?"

Jeesh, *I* didn't know. I'd never played pretend with other kids, just by myself.

I answered Kate: "Maybe I can be king."

Kate shook her head firmly. "Our father is the king."

Jango stubbed at the scrawny grass. "Kate says he's on crusade."

"He *is* on crusade," Kate shot back.

In the time I'd been at the Torgles', the twins' dad hadn't bothered to call or write. On crusade. Right.

"He's gone," muttered Jango.

"Ben!" Kate yelled, as if trying to drown out Jango's words. "You could be a fairy like the Barbies—"

"No," I said firmly. "How about a prince?"

Kate giggled. "Then Princess Lenora has to kiss you."

Jango turned all shades of pink.

"Why?" I asked. I wasn't sure I could stomach a kiss from a seven-year-old—even to help Grover.

"Why?" Kate repeated. "Be*cause* . . . that's what the king commands."

Jango's face went as red as the tights on her head, but she still didn't say a word. Do this, do that: Kate bossed and Jango obeyed. If Kate wanted to wear pink, they both wore pink. If Kate wanted to watch TV, they both watched

TV. If Kate spun a fairy tale about her deadbeat dad, Jango had to spin, too. Kate the Great needed to hear a few *no*s.

I pointed to the noble steed, who was gently panting. "Charmaine is the only one allowed to kiss me."

This time it was Jango who giggled.

"Oh, all right," Kate humphed. She peeled four strands of tinsel from the tree, decorated my shoulders, then stepped back.

"A knight in shining armor," she pronounced.

Luckily, a knight didn't have to do much but stand with the scratching steed. Around me, the twins prepared a feast for the absent king. Well, actually, Kate plucked the greenest grass—rare as gold in this pitiful yard—while Jango fingered a leaf here, a brown blade there, but added nothing to the dishrag Kate called "the Royal Plate."

Casually I dropped my first question: "Do you think Tracey will visit soon?"

Kate instantly stopped her grand preparations. "Why?" She batted her lashes. "Do you like her?"

I shrugged. "Just thought you might know something"—I coolly brushed at my tinsel—"but obviously you don't."

Of course, Kate couldn't miss an opportunity to show off her teeny bit of knowledge. It took a while to untangle the twins' story, filled with more gaps than Grover's grin. You could tell the girls had put together the whole tale from eavesdropping on the Torgles. To hear them tell it, Tracey had just up and left one day. Disappeared, leaving Grover behind while her boyfriend slept. He didn't know what to do with Grover because the baby wasn't his. (The twins got confused here but I knew what was going on.

The guy wasn't Grover's real father and couldn't be bothered with him.) Tracey's older sister, Jenny, worked during the day and went to college at night. And so Grover had been thrown to the system.

I remembered how I got started in the system. It was the morning Gram fell. I remembered hearing the crash and running into the kitchen. Gram was lying beside a tipped-over chair. "I can't, Ben," she whispered when I tried to help her get up. Her poor hands scrabbled at the floor. "Oh, Jesus, I can't." That scared me. Gram was never one to toss around the Lord's name. I brought her a towel, wet and folded, just like she asked, and she pressed it to her face. I brought her the phone and she dialed 911. When the ambulance came and they loaded her up, Gram grabbed tight hold of my hands. "I'll be gone a little while," she promised, "and come back good as new."

I smelled Ben-gay, warm and sharp, on my hands when I lifted them to my eyes.

Things after that are all mixed up. I'm not sure what happened when. A woman—a social worker, I learned later—put me in the backseat of a blue car. I was worried about Gram's false teeth, still in their night cup. How would Gram eat? How would she smile? But the car moved very fast. It took me to a cluttered office with green walls. I waited while the woman wrote on the blank lines of many pieces of paper. Then I was taken to a house. Someone made me a sandwich. Peanut butter. But it wasn't Jif.

Gram died the next day. The social worker came to the strange house and told me. She used easy words—"broken hip," "very old," "lots of pain"—but I didn't understand, not then. Not till the funeral.

The social worker held my hand the whole time, but I wasn't scared. I felt I was watching everything from far away. There was Gram, still and quiet inside that big box. That was strange. She had always been one to sniffle and snuffle and snore through the night. She looked nice, though, with her white hair smooth, not all wispy. I heard the preacher dropping his words, one by one, into the church silence. When he started thanking the Lord for Gram's long life, for her eighty-two good years on Earth, I almost fell over. Eighty-two! Gram was old. She had no business standing on that kitchen chair, I thought. I looked at her hands, bent with arthritis, while the social worker's, slim and warm, grasped my own. Whatever Gram had wanted, whatever she needed from the highest shelf, I wished she had asked. I would have fetched it for her.

After the funeral the system tried to trace my mother. Nothing. They had no record of my father. The woman told me Gram's will left me to the care of a friend, who'd gone into a nursing home that spring. So the system sent me to my first foster home. Number One, a transition home. Short stay, you're on your way. To Number Two.

The Crawdiches had thought about adoption before I arrived. I was on trial—and failed. Too many time-outs in the closet. By the time I left, I was six years old. Quiet and serious. Not an easy kid to find a home for. Most folks want a bouncing baby.

And Grover was that kind of baby. He had more bounce than a bucket of balls. Now he was at his own Number One with the Torgles. Who knew what would happen to him next? If his mother had stayed away, I bet he would have been adopted right off. Any grown-up would go gaga over him. Would love pinching his cheeks and playing piggy-wiggy with his toes. Would love showing off his picture in a big, fancy frame.

But his mother had returned. Returned and wanted him back.

That might seem like something to celebrate—unless you knew a few mothers who'd lost their kids to the system. Drinkers, most of them. Quick to yell and slap and wallop with a belt. Quick to walk out on their kids, just like Tracey.

Kate broke into my thoughts. "Tracey's pulling herself together, that's what Mrs. T. says. She's living with her sister."

"She's doing her best," said Jango.

Right. A girl like that was bound to disappear again, drink, do drugs, laze away any job she might land.

And Grover would be stuck with her—or back in the system. What kind of life was that?

I cleared my throat for one last question, something I'd wondered about for a while. "The *G* in Grover G. Graham—what does it stand for?"

Kate pondered the question. "Gumball," she giggled.

What a ditz.

I'd found out all I needed to know, but I continued playing knight for a while. It was almost fun, once I knew what to do. Basically I bowed when Jango curtsied (which thankfully wasn't too often) and watched while Kate twirled and thumped through what she called "The King's Welcome Dance." Pitiful. All for a man on permanent crusade. When Kate finally finished, I let myself clap loud and long for her.

After dinner, Ms. Burkell called. She was sorry, but the Number Nine they had lined up—a wonderful young couple—hadn't worked out. I pictured the bounce-bounce-bounce of her hair beads. "I know these temporary arrangements are hard, Ben. I promise, we'll have you settled soon."

A young couple. Maybe they were as kissy as Kitty and Ken. At least with the Torgles I wasn't worried about interrupting anything. At their age, they were all kissed out.

Ms. Burkell cleared her throat. She was working up to some "meaningful contact."

"Would you like us to try to trace your mother again? It's been five—"

"No."

"It's a chance for a home with a relative."

"No."

"Are you afraid she might disappear again?"

Ms. Burkell was trying to get into my head. I knew how to handle that. Just keep saying no.

Sarah Jewel had never called, never written. She didn't even know Gram was dead.

Snooping can get you in *big* trouble, that's what I kept telling the twins. I'd take my own advice, thank you very much. Sarah Jewel wanted to forget she had a kid. Fine. I wouldn't give her a reason to remember.

I thought about Grover. About Tracey beaming in and out of his life like some fairy god-awful mother. Ms. Burkell might want to spin a sweet tale about Sarah Jewel's return, the kind Kate spun about her dad, but I would refuse to listen.

Ms. Burkell sighed. "I'll find you a new place soon."

As I hung up I wondered *exactly* how much time "temporary" included. Three weeks, four weeks, six? My shortest stay had been five weeks with Number One. So far I'd been four weeks with the Torgles.

Chapter Ten

The next week Grover's behavior changed. I never knew such a kid for acting one way one day and a different way the next. That's how it is with babies, I guess. Always learning some new thing. Must be why they have those huge Tweety Bird heads—to fit everything in.

Anyway, just like that, Grover started dropping things. Mrs. T. would set him in his high chair and spread bits of hot dog on the tray. *Plop! Plop! Plop!* In two seconds they'd be on the floor.

He dropped stuffed toys out of his crib.

He dropped plastic toys out of his stroller.

He dropped magazines off the coffee table.

Plop! Plop! Plop!

Then he would bawl till you fetched them.

And don't you know, he'd drop them again.

At first this frazzled my nerves, but then I started to worry. Maybe he had a disease. Or defective fingers.

I checked his hands but they seemed okay. He could still get a good grasp on Charmaine's ears. And he could pinch my nose like the devil.

I worried about this for a few days—till I came across the Dr. Spock book in my sock drawer. I'd forgotten all about it.

Baby and Child Care was chockful of teeny print and a few cartoon pictures. It would take forever to read this whole book. But in the back was an index, and luckily, *dropping* was listed.

So I turned the yellowed pages and read the teeny print and—how about that!—Grover was doing just the right thing. The book said dropping was an important skill.

I flipped through a few more pages. Yeah, this could give me a big jump on Grover. I read about throwing and teething and feeding and napping. There was even a section on toilet training, which I skipped over. I sure wasn't going to teach him the potty.

That evening at dinner Grover tossed a french fry and hit Kate on the arm. When she hollered, I trotted out my new knowledge. "Grover's practicing his throwing and dropping," I explained. "That's how he learns, you know."

"Yeah?" Kate fielded another fry. "Well, when is he going to learn to clean up?"

"That comes later," I said.

"*Much* later, apparently." Mr. T. was pointing at Kate's jacket on the floor when—*bonk!*—a fry caught him square on the nose.

That set everyone off. Mr. T. started laughing, which shook his whole self. The dog barked. The twins squealed. *Bang!* went Grover's spoon. And from the kitchen, where she was fetching dessert, Mrs. T. hollered, "What am I missing?"

Then there was a crash.

In the silence, the clock went *tick . . . tick . . . tick*. Then—*scriitch*—Mr. T. pushed back his chair and everyone ran for the kitchen. On the floor were jagged bits of broken bowl, blobs of red Jell-O, and Mrs. T.

"Ahhh, Eileen," Mr. T. murmured, kneeling beside his wife.

The twins turned scared eyes to me. Like *I* knew what to do.

Slowly I made my way to the sink. A fall, I thought. A bone could be broken. Maybe her hip like Gram. What if Mrs. T. couldn't get up?

I remembered Gram's fingers, bent as bird claws, holding a wet cloth to her face.

I grabbed a clean dishrag and turned on the faucet. The cold water woke up my hands. Woke them into wringing and folding and passing that cloth to Mr. T. He pressed it gently to his wife's closed eyes.

Bang! I heard from the next room. Grover! The little guy was still carrying on with his spoon and french fries. I wheeled his high chair into the kitchen so I could keep an eye on him.

"Ga," he shouted. Drool dripped from his chin.

Mrs. T. finally jerked and opened her eyes. Jeesh, she looked white.

"What happened?" She blinked. "I remember lifting the bowl, then my back—" She winced. "I must have blacked out for a moment."

When Mrs. T. tried to stand, she gasped and her knees

buckled. She would have fallen again if Mr. T. hadn't gripped her arm.

"How can I put my back out just *lifting* a bowl?"

"It's the angle you do the lifting." Mr. T. loomed over his small wife. Frankenstein and Flea. I felt ashamed of the names I'd first called them.

"You need to be more careful," Mr. T. went on. "Don't worry, I'll clean this up."

"Better sooner than later." Mrs. T. tried to make a joke, then slapped some tone into her voice. "Now, please quit fussing and get me back to the table."

But Mrs. T.'s tone wasn't going to work with her husband. Mr. T. said he was taking her straight to bed. On the stairs, their footsteps sounded heavy and slow.

The twins started to cry.

"Ga!" yelled Grover, flinging fries.

I wished Mrs. T. hadn't fallen. What had happened to her back? What if she had to go to the hospital?

As the twins sniffled I took a deep breath. Boo-hooing and blabbing wouldn't change a thing. I'd learned that in the system. Keep moving, keep doing—that got you through. "Jango," I said, "clean off the table. Kate, you load the dishwasher."

The tears stopped. "It's Jango's turn to load," said Kate.

"Do it," I said.

Then I turned to Grover. He was bashing a fry on his head and wearing half of his dinner. One teeny washcloth wouldn't make a dent in that mess. Carefully I hoisted him out of his high chair and hauled him to the bathroom. While I shimmied him out of his clothes, Grover tossed every shampoo bottle into the tub. Who cared? They were plastic. They floated. They kept him busy while I scrubbed his hair.

When he was bathed and dried and squeezed into his diaper and pajamas, Grover turned bright eyes to me and commanded: "Ba." *Hop on Pop*. The little con man figured he'd delay bedtime. But I gave him only two readings. Dr. Spock thinks limits are important.

Downstairs the twins were sitting at the table, big eyes on me as I entered.

"Mrs. T.?" Jango asked.

I tried to put some bounce in my voice. "Mrs. T. . . . um," I replied. "She's going to be okay."

Kate stared me down. "Mrs. T. has cancer," she said.

"Cancer? No," I said, startled. "Mrs. T. hurt her back."

"Cancer gets everything." Jango stuck her doll in her mouth. "Lung cancer. Breast cancer. Mrs. T. probably has back cancer."

The twins looked pretty shook up.

Keep moving, keep doing—that kept me from worrying. Maybe it would work for them.

"Everything will be okay," I said, then borrowed some tone from Mrs. T.: "Upstairs, now. Bathtime."

"But—"

"And then bed."

"But—"

"No buts. Go."

And they went.

Later when I checked, I found the girls curled up in their beds, with the light still burning bright. I could hear Kate sniffing and Jango softly chewing. Their sounds reminded me of Gram's nightly snuffles and snores.

I spoke softly: "Mrs. T. is going to be okay."

"Are you sure?" Kate asked.

"Pretty sure," I said.

"My daddy would know *for sure*."

I didn't say a word about deadbeat fathers. Jango had her Barbie's feet; Kate had her dream daddy. I had my goals laid out A, B, C. Whatever got you through. I clicked off the switch but left the door slightly open so some light from the hall could shine in. Even a teeny glow can help if you wake up scared in the night.

I figured I'd better stay awake in case Mr. and Mrs. T. needed to go to the hospital or something, so I propped myself on the couch with *Where Eagles Dare*. My eyeballs were so tuckered out the words kind of tangled together. From what I could tell, an American general had been captured by the enemy. The main character planned to rescue the man . . . kidnap him.

"Thought you'd be in bed by now."

Jeesh, I must have dozed off. I blinked up at Mr. T.

He told me he had tried to get his wife resting easy with a heating pad and back rub. Whoa, Ben-gay! The smell was so strong my eyes suddenly stung. I remembered Gram smoothing the white lotion into her hands, then slowly twisting the lid off the Jif jar.

"Strained back," Mr. T. said, stretching. "Did it myself once, lifting a bin of nails. I was flat on my back for a week. Helpless as a baby."

"A *baby*?" I said. "Grover is the least helpless person I know."

It wasn't a very good joke—like Gram, I'd never been much good at jokes—but Mr. T. let out a big laugh. Maybe it was relief or something. I was feeling that way myself.

"Ahhh." Tonight Mr. T.'s "ahhh" sounded tired. "The problem is"—the man sat down beside me—"Eileen won't like lying flat on her back. It's what she needs to get well, but first chance she gets, she'll want to be up and about. Checking on Grover. Keeping track of the girls. I've convinced her to stay put tomorrow." He sighed. "Who knows what she'll be up to the rest of the week."

Mr. T. mentioned he'd call a baby-sitter to stay with Grover tomorrow. "I have to leave for work by seven," he said, "but I don't think I can get a sitter to come any earlier than eight. Will you and the girls be okay?"

I nodded, then added: "The twins seem pretty upset." With Mr. T. somehow I didn't feel I was squealing. "They think Mrs. T. might have cancer."

"Their mother died of cancer." Mr. T. cleared his throat. "They in bed?"

I nodded again.

"We'll talk to them tomorrow." He pinched the space between his eyes. "I wish I could take tomorrow off, but I can't on such short notice. They had to let another guy go at the store yesterday." Mr. T. ran his hand over his face. "That new hardware store on Route Three is killing us. Everyone wants to buy there."

Mr. T. tried to slap a smile over his worried look. "Guess the best thing for us both is some shut-eye," he said. "I'm going to sleep on the couch so Eileen can rest better."

As I scrambled off his sleeping place I kept pushing a thought out of my brain. Only when I entered Jake's room and settled into Jake's bed did I let myself puzzle over Mr. T.'s words.

The man had talked like I was someone who knew

the place and the people. Someone who was not a stray, or even a guest. Someone who might stick around.

I knew that wasn't true. I was temporary. Short stay, I'm on my way. I fiddled with my night-light and then lay back. Tomorrow I'd blank out Mr. T.'s words. For now, it felt kind of nice to let them float in my head.

Chapter Eleven

Plop! crash! bang! jerked me awake. It sounded like an invasion.

Then came an excited squeal.

Grover. Tossing and dropping.

I squinted at the bedside clock. 7:10 A.M.

"Why," I muttered, stumbling to Grover's room, "can't you learn a *quiet* skill?"

Grover flashed a huge smile. "Ba! Ba!" he cried, jerking his crib bars, head swaying like a happy bear's. He flapped his fist. You would think he'd been watching for me his whole life.

But I knew it wasn't me he was happy to see. Oh, no. He was happy to see Plastic Doughnut, Squeaky Mouse, and Lambie Pie. All the toys he'd tossed to the floor, which I put back into his crib.

He started to toss them again.

"Shhh, Grover." I hoisted him out of the crib. "You'll wake up Mrs. T."

"Ga-ba." Grover dived for my nose.

Jeesh, was he ripe! I contemplated sticking him back in his crib and waiting for the sitter. After all, she got paid to deal with this.

But that stinky diaper was starting to sag. And the way he was prancing, he'd soon have poop all over his pajamas and sheet. All over Plastic Doughnut, Squeaky Mouse, and Lambie Pie.

So I stuck him on the changing table. He squirmed like he'd been clamped to a bed of nails. By this time I had an audience of two—Kate and Jango—trying to talk, double fast, double loud, over Grover's squeals. Somehow I managed to puff out some baby powder and fasten a diaper, just in time to hear Jango say, ". . . can't come."

"Who can't come?" I coughed, releasing Grover's stranglehold on my neck.

"The baby-sitter," the twins cried. "We already told you a million times."

"She's sick," explained Jango.

"We told her we'd take care of Mrs. T.," Kate added. "We're the best nurses in the world, that's what Mom always said."

So while I plunked Grover into his high chair, the twins set the kettle to boiling, and, at 7:45 A.M., fixed Mrs. T. a cup of instant chicken noodle soup. Even when I explained that Mrs. T. had a hurt back, not cancer, not a cold, the twins just blinked big eyes at me and said they knew what to do. They bustled out of the kitchen like two Clara Bartons, with a tray full of crackers and soup.

At least the twins left me free to deal with Grover. But

that bulldozer-vacuum baby needed a double-octopus sitter. I bet even sixteen arms couldn't keep up with him. Feed, clean, change, play, feed, clean, change, play, change. Hour after hour after hour. At least with Charmaine around I didn't have to sweep. She gobbled any food Grover threw to the floor.

By the time Mr. T. returned, I was flaked out on the couch, munching a peanut butter cracker, channel-grazing the afternoon TV. In their room, Kate and Jango were playing nurse with their Barbies and two white socks. I'd just managed to lay Grover down for a nap.

"Ahhh." Mr. T. lifted the brim of his cap. "Looks like you've had an easy day."

I bounced off that couch so fast I must have been a blur. Easy! Easy to change about forty dirty diapers!

"Just teasing." He smiled, then asked, "Where's the sitter?"

So I sat back and told him the story of my day with Grover. Feed, clean, change, play, feed, clean, change, play, change.

Mr. T. eyed my clothes. "Those your sleeping duds?"

I glanced down at my T-shirt, spotted with cereal from Grover's breakfast.

"Go change," he said. "I'll take over."

I headed to the shower and, minutes later, when *plop! crash! bang!* reached my ears, it sounded good to hear Mr. T's *thump . . . thump . . . thump* stop at Grover's room.

Before I went down to dinner, I opened my sock drawer and thumbed through the Dr. Spock book. Checking to make sure I hadn't messed up. The cartoons made me smile. Lots of get-into-everything babies and frazzle-haired moms.

But later I started wondering about the dads. Why weren't they in the pictures? Shoot, when Grover threw his mashed potatoes at dinner, Mr. T. looked frazzled enough for any cartoon.

Chapter Twelve

Mr. T. stayed home the next day, and together we managed to keep Grover from completely wrecking the place. The twins were about as helpful as two heart attacks, since all they did was play their usual games of pretend. At least I thought they were pretend until, passing through the living room, I heard Kate say fiercely, "He *is* coming back."

"You're a liar," said Jango.

"*You* are."

Uh-oh. Trouble in Twinville. Sounded like King Daddy had fallen from Jango's throne. And Kate was trying to shove him back.

"I can't hear yooouuuu." Jango clapped both hands to her ears.

"That's because I'm not talking to you," Kate shrilled.

A fight. How long would it last? Less than five minutes, I thought, heading for the kitchen. One twin didn't know how to act without the other.

While Grover napped, I decided to check out the dinner situation. Last night Mr. T. had created instant mashed potatoes that tasted like paste. Even the human vacuum cleaner flat-out refused to eat them. Grover had plopped them on his head like a white, lumpy cap.

I'm not bragging about my cooking, but I've scratched up a few meals in my time, especially at Number Seven, the Hartmans'. That house was not one for regular dinners since Kitty and Ken did not keep regular hours. They'd haul in groceries every two weeks and tell me to help myself. But soon I'd be stuck with the crumbs at the bottom of the chip bag. When I turned on the TV after school, my stomach rumbled with every food commercial. I swear I could smell noodles steaming and meat sizzling right through the tube.

To kill time, I'd mosey down to the Safeway and check out the free samples. Fancy crackers. Fruit on colored toothpicks. Cheese cubes the perfect size for popping into your mouth.

I learned not to take too much. People might notice and start asking questions. I remembered one woman feeding me sausage after tiny sausage from a heaped-high tray. I had just speared my sixth when she zoomed in on me. What was my name? Were my parents at home? Was I getting enough to eat? I backed away, swallowing fast. Avoided Safeway for the rest of the week.

And when I went back, I had cash—my school milk money and some change Kitty and Ken had left lying around. That's when I discovered the discount rack. Sure, the squashed muffins and dented cans looked pitiful, but the food tasted the same as the pretty stuff on the shelves. And it was half the price. Talk about bargains! For dinner

I'd open and eat one whole can. I loved fruit cocktail and corned beef hash.

I never tried to save on peanut butter, though. No cheap brands or smooth brown paste for me. Gram had always spread Jif, extra crunchy, on our saltines. The day I bought my first jar, turned the lid, and breathed deep— well, I felt like I was throwing myself a party. A *big* pick-me-up.

I even tried cooking—crinkle fries, tomato soup, fish sticks. I'd search the Safeway for stuff served at the school cafeteria and try to copy it. Pancakes were my favorite, though—maybe because Gram used to make them. I loved to measure the mix, add water, stir, pour, flip—just like Gram. She used to cook up huge stacks of teeny circles she called silver dollars. I remembered the smell grabbing me hard by the nose and hauling me fast to the table.

The trouble with making silver dollars myself, though, was that the first was stone-cold by the time I flipped the last. At Number Seven, I learned to make one giant pancake that filled the whole pan. And if it broke when I flipped it or was raw in the middle, I'd dress it up with extra Log Cabin syrup. It tasted just as good.

Rummaging through the Torgles' kitchen cabinets, all I could think of was pancakes. Thick. Sweet. Sticky.

When Mr. T. sent the twins to set the table, Kate fussed about my spatula and pan.

"Ben," she yelled, "you're making breakfast for dinner."

"Ben," Jango yelled louder, "you're making binner."

"Ben!" Kate screamed. "Dreakfast!"

What was *wrong* with these two? They were Ben-ing like Ms. Burkell.

Then it hit me. I was to be the go-between during their fight. Kate and Jango planned to say *everything* to me. Their usual chatter was bad enough, but this competing chatter—chaos with a capital *C*.

"BEN!" they both hollered.

By this time the pancake smell was wafting through the house. It brought Mr. T., with Grover in his arms. It got Kate and Jango competing for the first brown circle. It even roused a request from Mrs. T. upstairs for "just a little bite."

You should have seen Grover tuck into his meal! He scooped up those pancakes like a baby bulldozer and sucked them down like a high-speed vacuum.

By the time I sat down with my one giant pancake and the big jug of syrup, the table was empty. For once the girls had gone their separate ways. Mr. T. had swooped Grover off to the tub.

As I ate I watched night slowly fill up the window. If lonesome had a color, I thought, this was it. A gray growing steadily darker.

But then the first few stars gleamed through. I thought of Gram. I thought of her favorite joke. I thought of her teeth coming out at night.

I wished I could remember more things about Gram. I squeezed my eyes shut and concentrated real hard—but the same bits kept showing up. False teeth. Jif. Silver-dollar pancakes. I wished I had something from her home. Like those little horse shakers I'd played with. It would be nice to hold something that once belonged to Gram.

I heard the house lights click on. In the next room, the twins' chitchat hummed like summer bugs. I guessed their

71

fight was over. Grover gobble-gurgled like a happy turkey: "Ga-ba-da."

I listened for a while and then I cleaned up.

Mr. T. and I became a team that week. We wouldn't wow the National Football League, but we managed to get things done. With Mrs. T. laid up, I took over dinner. The hard part was deciding what to make. Rice-A-Roni or hash? Instant pudding or Jell-O? Cooking at the Hartmans' had been easy. There was no choice. Tang, chips, and a margarine stick—that was it. But the Torgles' kitchen was a miniature Safeway. I could fix something different each night.

Friday while I was cooking, Ms. Burkell called.

"The Torgles told me you've been a big help," she said.

I listened while I stirred pancake mix with one hand, held the phone with the other, watched Grover gnaw his tippy-cup, tried to tune out the twins, and steadied the leg Charmaine was whacking with her tail.

I remembered my last talk with Ms. Burkell. I waited for Sarah Jewel to come up again.

Instead Ms. Burkell said, "I hear you're great with babies. Are you having fun?"

Grover glanced at me, grinned, and began shaking his cup. Milk rained from the teeny holes.

"Fun," I said, "is not the word."

Ms. Burkell laughed. "At your next home," she said, "I can try to place you with young children, if you'd like."

At my next home. That was right. I was temporary.

Something swelled in my chest. I pushed it down.

I listened to Ms. Burkell apologize for the slow progress on Number Nine.

I swallowed. "I'm used to it," I said.

Ms. Burkell trotted out a few more "I'm sorry's." I wanted to ask if the Torgles had said anything about me staying longer. What if they wanted me to live there past the summer? What if they wanted me to continue to help? Could the system change its plans?

Ms. Burkell interrupted my thoughts. "With the new shopping center pulling business away from downtown Greenfield," she said, "things must be uncertain for the Torgles."

"Uncertain"? What did that mean? Would Mr. T. lose his job? Were the Torgles hurting for money?

"Ga-ba-da," murmured Grover. Somehow he had pried the lid off his tippy-cup. Milk flooded across the floor.

"Whee!" He splashed in the white puddle while Charmaine licked his toes. Of course the twins did nothing but squeal.

"I better go," I said, hanging up.

Mopping the mess, with Charmaine's help, I thought about Ms. Burkell. I bet her hair beads bounce-bounce-bounced all cheery no matter what she said. *At your next home. At your next home.* Those words stuck in my head.

No foster home had ever asked me to stay. The Torgles might be too busy with the girls and Grover; they might not want another kid when school started. And if money was tight, maybe they couldn't afford to keep someone who was just temporary. I took a deep breath. The end of summer was far away. I decided to be like Ms. Burkell's beads. For once I would not think ahead; I'd just sort of bounce along.

Late that evening Mrs. T. got a call. She was downstairs, telling everyone she felt fine, then wincing when she thought no one was looking.

When she hung up, Mrs. T. told us Tracey would be coming to visit. In two days. On Sunday afternoon.

Chapter Thirteen

The day before Tracey arrived, though, Grover started into his best skill of all. Grover learned to talk.

Dropping and throwing, well, those skills could get on your nerves. He still had no manners at meals.

But after dinner Saturday when I plopped down in our usual *Hop on Pop* spot, Grover came toddling up. "Ben," he said. "Ben."

Actually, it sounded more like "Beh." But that was still very different from his usual "ba."

"Beh! Beh!" Grover climbed beside me.

"Ahhh." Mr. T. peered over the newspaper. "How about that? The baby just said his first word."

"Beh! Beh! Beh!"

Some sort of spotlight clicked on inside me then. My heart and chest—I bet they were glowing.

Of course Kate and Jango had to get into the act, trying to teach Grover their names.

The kid bounced beside me on the couch. "Beh! Beh! Beh!"

I couldn't help grinning as I opened *Hop on Pop*. The book was as boring as ever but for once that didn't bug me.

The next morning, Grover added a new word, *bye,* to go with his flapped fist, which still meant both "hello" and "good-bye."

But he hadn't forgotten *Beh*. It was "Beh" when I hoisted him out of his crib and "Beh" when I fed him his goop. In fact, "Beh" followed me around for the rest of the day, just like *swish, swish, swish.*

Before Tracey came over, I scoured the living-room rug for the teeniest bit of popcorn or fuzz, for any dropped rubber bands. I knew Grover's vacuum-cleaner self would gobble any small thing in his path. Who could trust Tracey to remove it before he choked?

When the knock came, the twins raced to the front door, let Tracey in, and watched to see where she put her purse. Dying to check out the new makeup, I bet. Mrs. T. fussed over Tracey, asking how she felt, as they headed toward the living room.

"Grover's taking a nap," she explained while Tracey eyed the blanket on the (ultraclean) rug. I had placed Lambie Pie in the middle so the kid would have a buddy close by.

"When will he wake up?" Tracey checked her watch. "I can only stay a couple of hours. My sister—"

A couple of hours. And she hadn't seen Grover in almost two weeks.

"He just went to sleep," I declared from the doorway. "You shouldn't wake him up."

Dr. Spock says little kids need lots of sleep.

Tracey looked me up, down.

"Who's that?" She jerked a chin in my direction.

"Ben lives here," said Mrs. T., directing a voice chockful of tone at me. "And he was about to leave."

No, I wasn't.

Tracey didn't bother to glance my way again. She looked dead white and tired. She better not pass on any germs to the baby.

"Grover—" she began.

Just then *plop! crash! bang!* came from upstairs.

I raced to get Grover, but when I brought him downstairs, still sleepy-smiley, and Tracey held out her arms, Grover shied away. He stuck his nose in my neck.

"What's wrong?" Tracey asked sharply.

"Beh! Beh!" Grover cried.

Mrs. T. tried to distract him with Lambie Pie, but Grover batted it back. When Tracey took him, he stiffened and screamed.

"Grover," soothed Mrs. T., shaking the lamb. "It's your mommy. Mommy's here."

She motioned me to leave, so I backed up. Very slowly. I kept my eyes on Tracey. I saw the anger in her blue eyes, but I kept mine drilled hard to hers. Let her see I knew all about her. How she had treated Grover. Left him. Ran away.

I refused to look away.

For the next two hours, I stayed close to that living room. In the hall, out of sight, but watchful. Mrs. T. drifted in and out, doing a lousy job of supervising. Once she arched her brows at me and shook her head. But she didn't say anything. That was good. I wasn't about to leave Grover alone with that girl.

After a while Grover settled down, though he sometimes whimpered, "Beh." He fiddled with Lambie Pie's yellow bow.

Tracey didn't seem to know what to do with her kid. She didn't have a clue how to play, how to talk. She didn't make Lambie Pie tickle Grover's toes. (That makes him laugh.) She didn't cry "baa, baa." (That sets him baaing, too.)

I wondered what Dr. Spock would say about Tracey. I figured she was hopeless. Grover would be better off without her.

I wished she would disappear, just like Sarah Jewel.

Chapter Fourteen

In the next few weeks Tracey visited three times each week. On those days the house was chaos with *all* capital letters: *C-H-A-O-S*.

Grover spilled more, Charmaine barked more, and the twins giggled and whined and screamed four times louder than usual. Mrs. T. praised every little mother thing Tracey managed to do right. I watched for each wrong one.

And one day, to add to the chaos, Tracey brought her sister.

I'd just plunked Grover in his high chair, where he started squashing green beans in his hair. Charmaine was stationed below, munching the falling bits.

And in sailed Tracey, like she owned the place, with some woman trailing behind. Tracey took one look at Grover's plate, opened her pouty lips, and bellowed, "He needs fruit."

"Grover had a banana this morning," I replied, handing him another green bean.

"Na-na!" Grover hollered.

Mrs. T. stopped by with a basket full of dirty clothes. Toting that heavy thing, she would hurt her back again, for sure. "You two"—Mrs. T. leveled some tone at Tracey and me—"feeding Grover is *not* a contest."

So I *very* politely gave Tracey my seat and watched her chop up a banana. She had painted blue moons on each one of her fingernails. How dumb.

Tracey dumped the banana slices on Grover's plate. Right on the picture of Peter Rabbit.

Big mistake. Grover likes to chat with Peter while he eats. The banana didn't stay on the plate for long.

Plop! Plop! Plop! Grover peeked over the edge of his high chair. "Na-na," he crowed. "Bye."

I didn't try to hide my grin.

Kate skipped in and skidded. "What a mess!"

Tracey leaned over and scraped banana goop off Kate's shoe. "That's how Grover learns," she sighed.

"Ben says that, too." Jango entered, also skidding. I noticed that her yellow T-shirt was completely different from Kate's pink-flowered top. Was Jango rebelling against Kate the Great?

"Beh! Beh!" Grover gobbled a bean.

"*Ben,*" muttered Tracey.

Mrs. T. whisked off Grover's gooey bib and popped it in the laundry basket. She pointed to Tracey. "Ma-ma," she said, slowly and clearly. "Ma-ma."

Grover looked up from patting Jango's shirt. "El," he said.

"Yellow," repeated Mrs. T. "Jango's yellow shirt. Grover, listen. Can you say 'Mama'?"

"Ma-ma," Grover obliged.

Tracey sucked in her breath. She looked like she was going to cry or something. Jeesh. Grover was just repeating a word.

"Ma-ma," Grover said again.

"Your fingernails!" Kate screeched, grabbing Tracey's hand. "Let me see."

"Shhh," whispered Tracey. "Grover, come to Mama?"

She didn't even wait for the baby to hold out his arms. Just hauled him out of the high chair and announced, sailing out the door, that *she* would put him down for a nap.

Following with her basket, Mrs. T. smiled at Tracey. "And you thought Grover didn't know his own mother."

"We want moons, too!" Kate hollered as she and Jango skipped after Tracey, with Charmaine skittering behind.

Suddenly the dining room was quiet. I picked a few green beans off Grover's tray.

"You must be Ben," came a low voice. "Tracey told me about you."

Ha, I thought. I bet she had said nothing good.

"I'm Jenny. Tracey's sister."

I continued to clean, giving the woman a side-eyes glance. Short hair. No pouty lips. No spider lashes.

This was Tracey's sister? Tracey's tight clothes and makeup screamed, "Look at me!" but Jenny, with her plain shirt and plain face . . . well, Jenny seemed to blend in.

The woman wiped squished banana off the floor. Tracey would never have done that. She'd cut out every single blue moon from her fingernails before she would stoop to help me.

"You two sure seem different," I said.

Jenny gave me a little smile—and you could tell she didn't smile often. "I'm the quiet one," she said, screwing the lid on Grover's baby-food jar of green beans. "Tracey, on the other hand . . . I remember my mother saying that even as a baby Tracey had no trouble letting her feelings out."

Tracey as a baby. With big blue eyes and a Tweety Bird head and fat little fists like Grover's. What a weird thought. I wondered what I'd been like as a baby. What my mother—what Sarah Jewel might have said about me.

"But we've both got a stubborn streak," Jenny continued, wiping the table while I wiped the high chair. "When we make up our mind—that's it. Tracey used to smoke about two packs a day. As soon as she found out she was pregnant—not a puff. Didn't want to hurt her baby."

Well, she hurt him anyway. What would you call running away?

Jenny gave *me* a side-eyes glance. "I bet you've got a stubborn streak, Ben."

Me? I thought about Gram sticking it out with her Ben-gay

and great-grandbaby. Doing the whole feed-change-play thing with me. *That* was stubborn.

And Jenny was seeing some of that stubborn in me. Huh. Maybe I had a bit of Gram's spirit inside. More than just memories of false teeth and Jif.

"What are you stubborn about?" I asked.

"Right now? Finishing college, even though going part-time takes forever." Jenny continued to wipe the table. "And sometimes," she went on, "I'm just plain mule-ornery *stubborn*." She shook her head. "Stubborn can make you tough," she sighed, "or it can make you hard. There's a difference."

Tracey's stubborn streak had made her hard. I could tell. *You been raised by a perfect mama?* That girl liked being flat-out mean.

"Tracey is—" Jenny began.

"Tracey is *what*?" Tracey surveyed us from the doorway. Her eyes moved from Jenny to me back to Jenny, like someone left out of a secret.

The twins squeezed past her. Their fingers fluttered like hyper butterflies. "Moons! Moons! Tracey made us moons!"

The chaos was starting again.

Plop! crash! bang! came from upstairs.

"Your baby's calling, Mama," Jenny teased.

"Grover just went to sleep," Tracey sighed, "and now he's playing dropsy."

"That's how he learns." Jango poked a painted finger-nail into my rib. "Right, Ben?"

Tracey frowned, than turned suddenly to Jenny. "What

were you talking about?" she demanded. "Tracey is *what?*"

"Wonderful," Jenny said lightly.

"Ha!" Tracey's laugh was bitter. "Like you or *he* would think that."

Chapter Fifteen

As if Tracey's visits weren't enough, Mrs. T. had to plan what she called a "family picnic" for the third Saturday in July. I almost faked a stomachache when I found out Tracey was going. But if I stayed home, who would watch Grover?

Of course it was 94 sweaty degrees when we set off for Greenfield's not-so-green park. But with all us "family" wedged inside the car, the temperature must have hit 110. As usual, Mrs. T. reminded her husband to *please* fix that jiggling door and as usual he agreed. "Better sooner than later," she humphed.

I watched a few sweetgums through the car window.

"Twee!" Grover pointed.

"That's right," I replied. "Tree."

"Twee," Grover repeated.

Behind sunglasses, Tracey's face showed no expression.

I wished Jenny could have come, but she was studying for an exam. She said she wanted to finish college early, even if that meant studying the whole summer away. Shoot, she must be plenty stubborn to get through all those books. They were thicker than Dr. Spock's *Baby and Child Care*! On one of her visits Jenny had even asked if I planned to go to college. Me? I shook my head no. I just wanted to get through A, B, and C on my list of goals; I didn't want to think about adding D.

The Torglemobile bounced over a rut and Tracey clutched at the cooler in her lap. Today she was proud as Red Riding Hood with a basket of goodies. Tracey had insisted on bringing the food, to save Mrs. T. the trouble, with her bad back and all. I wondered if she had remembered to pack Grover's favorite fish-shaped crackers.

Probably not.

When we reached the park, Kate, Jango, and Charmaine raced for the picnic tables. Tracey handed the cooler to Mr. T. and tried to unhook Grover's car seat.

She fiddled, tugged, twisted the strap.

I leaned over and—*click!*—unsnapped the catch.

Tracey's sunglasses briefly turned in my direction; then she picked up the baby.

"You're welcome," I said.

Mrs. T. frowned at me.

Let her frown. Someone had to watch out for the kid. His mother *still* didn't know what to do.

Mr. T. was already spreading a red-checked tablecloth and Kate was flinging paper plates on the table. Jango lifted plastic tubs from the cooler. Tiny triangle sandwiches. Potato salad. Chopped fruit with colored toothpicks.

Mrs. T. threw up her hands like a kid at Christmas. "What a beautiful picnic!"

"Do you like it?" Tracey smiled. "I tried to make it look like a picture I saw in *Ladies' Home Journal*."

Kate peeked inside a cookie tin. "Wow!"

The smell of homemade cookies made my mouth water, but I tried to blank out any interest.

Good thing I did. That picnic might have looked good, but it sure flunked the taste test. The bread was dry and the potato salad goopy. The cookies were hard as dirt clods.

"Jenny told me I wasn't measuring carefully—and Jenny is *always* right." Tracey tried to laugh, though her lips trembled. She crumbled a cookie. "At least I didn't mess up the fruit."

"Bish! Bish!" Grover hollered for his favorite fish crackers.

No one said a word about Tracey forgetting them. Mr. T. handed Grover a bread crust.

He threw it down. "Bish!" he demanded.

Mr. T. handed Grover a chunk of melon. "Why don't you all go to the playground? The swings might distract him."

The twins skipped off but Tracey held back. She didn't try to pick up Grover. Without the dark glasses, her eyes looked sort of sad.

Grover squished the melon till juice ran down his arm.

"Oh, Grover." Tracey grabbed a napkin.

He squealed and reached for me.

"Ben," Mrs. T. began, "why don't you stay here and let Tracey—" But then Grover set off and I had to skedaddle after. Tracey followed, her hand on Charmaine.

That dog would do anything for a pat.

At the playground, Kate and Jango were taking turns

with the whirl-go-round. One girl would push it fast, fast, fast while the other spun and shrieked.

The whirl-go-round. I've always hated that ride. What's the point of spinning till the whole world falls away? Till dizziness fills your head? I was once whirled so fast that I lost my grip. I remember my fingers slipping, the wind sucking hard. And then I was whirling and twirling through spinning air till the ground rose up and smacked me. I banged my head, scraped my shoulder, *and* up-chucked my lunch. Just watching the twins on that stupid ride made my stomach jump.

I herded Grover toward the swings.

"Tracey, spin us. Tracey, please!" Kate and Jango yelled, and soon their excited screams filled the air.

Grover toddled from swings to sandbox, but his busy eyes kept sliding in the direction of that big whirling thing.

"Ga." He pointed.

"Oh, Ben, let him ride." Kate brushed back her tangled bangs as the whirl-go-round slowed. "I'll hold him."

"He's too little—," I began.

"Sure, he can ride," Tracey broke in, clapping her hands at Grover. "Want to ride, baby? Come on!"

"Ga!" laughed Grover, clapping back.

"Come on, Grover!" yelled Kate.

Even Charmaine had to add her two cents' worth, barking like a fool.

And Grover? He toddled over so fast his stubby legs blurred.

Tracey picked up the baby and plunked him in Kate's lap. "Hold tight," she directed, starting to push.

Grover squealed and squirmed.

That dumb Kate. She wasn't paying attention.

In two strides, I was beside the whirl-go-round, reaching for Grover.

Tracey's voice stopped me. "He wants a ride."

I clenched my hands. I wished I were suddenly three inches taller. Then I could stare Tracey down. It's not the same when you have to stare up.

"That ride is dangerous," I said.

"Ben's afraid." Kate looked over at Tracey. "Listen. His voice is shaking."

Tracey shook her head. "You and Jenny," she said to me. "You're like two old bats, squeaky and scared." She grabbed a bar on the whirl-go-round. "This is *fun*."

"Whee!" Grover clapped his hands.

Tracey stared straight at me. "You're going to make Grover as nervous and sneaky as you. I don't want him to be like that."

My eyes didn't shift from hers. Listen to her, talking like I was hurting Grover. After what *she* had done. "What kind of mother are you?" My words came out, hot and hard. "You don't care. You left your baby—"

"What kind of mother am I?" Tracey's breath came fast, like mine. "I'm *Grover's* mother. And I say he's going to ride."

This must be some of Tracey's hard stubbornness. Well, I could be stubborn, too.

In one motion, I grabbed the bar, grabbed Grover from Kate. I plunked the baby on my lap.

"Ben's going to ride," cried the twins. "Tracey, make it go fast. Really fast!"

Tracey began pushing the ride.

"Faster," screamed Kate.

I hung on grimly to the bar, tightly to Grover.

The ride picked up speed.

"Faster!"

I watched Tracey's hands grab each bar and push. White hands, blue-dotted fingernails, gray steel bar. The green of leaves and grass spun together. Potato salad and cookies spun in my stomach.

"Bye!" Grover squealed, flapping his fist. "Bye!"

His hair whipped my cheek. I tightened my grip. I wanted to close my eyes, but I didn't. White-blue-gray-green-green-green. I tried to focus on the names of colors.

I will *not* get sick, I thought fiercely.

Then the whirl-go-round started slowing.

"What a short ride," whined Kate.

"And way too slow," Jango added her whine. "Come on, Tracey, spin us again."

"I wanted it slow and easy for Grover." Tracey stopped the ride. "Did you like that, baby boy?"

"Whee!" Grover laughed.

I didn't bother to look at Tracey. Stupid. Mean. Hard. Slow and easy for Grover. Like she cared.

I heaved the baby into my arms and stalked back to the picnic area. The potato salad and cookies fought in my stomach. A lousy mother *and* a lousy cook, I fumed, hearing the ride creak and the twins squeal and Charmaine excitedly bark.

I am *not* a squeaky old bat.

Mr. T. was stretched out in the shade, but Mrs. T. waved me to the table. I put Grover down, keeping an eye on him as I sat beside her.

Mrs. T. was smoothing crumbs to the edge of the table. The crumbs from Tracey's lousy cookies.

"Ben, you're great with Grover," she said slowly. "And he obviously loves you."

I smiled.

Mrs. T. pushed the crumbs into a neat pile. "But you seem . . . well, too protective when Tracey is around. Maybe you should step back a bit and let his mother take over."

I stiffened and blanked out my smile.

"You and Tracey"—Mrs. T. flattened the crumb pile—"seem to compete over the baby. Why don't you try helping her instead? Show her how to play with Grover, how to talk to him."

Me help Tracey? Ha. She wouldn't listen to one word I said. *You an expert?* I remembered her sneering. And why should I help her, anyway? I wasn't the one who had started the meanness.

"If you helped Tracey"—Mrs. T. looked straight at me—"don't you think you'd be helping Grover, too?"

I blanked out her words. Even if Tracey had a thousand helpers, she'd never be good for Grover. Too protective? How could I be too protective? Okay, so the whirl-go-round hadn't hurt Grover. And to hear the twins, maybe Tracey had pushed sort of slow. But Mrs. T. wanted me to step back. She wanted me to blend into the background like some camouflage fish. She wanted Tracey to take over—and me to be one big nothing in Grover's life.

Mrs. T. continued. "Tracey's been knocked around a lot. Her mom and dad were killed in a car accident when she was fourteen."

Well, I didn't have parents, either. So what? Everyone has a boo-hoo story.

"Jenny tried to take over, but she was only eighteen, working long hours, going to college at night. Tracey got in with the wrong people, people older than her. She was five months along before she realized she was pregnant."

Stupid. Stupid girl.

Mrs. T. studied me a moment, then sighed. "Why are you so hard on Tracey?"

You been raised by a perfect mama? No, but I sure recognized imperfect. Maybe I was hard because Mrs. T. was so soft. Someone had to look out for Grover.

Chapter Sixteen

Over the next few weeks Traccy continued to visit. Too often, if you ask me. After facing off at the whirl-go-round, we barely spoke. She finished her child care class and was considered fit to take her baby. The system was spitting Grover back.

We planned a party for the night before he left. Streamers. Presents. Mr. T. tied a yellow balloon to the high chair. It said Bon Voyage in red letters. Mrs. T. cooked a big cake and a teeny one and swirled white frosting over the tops.

"Chocolate's not good for babies," she said when the twins whined for fudge frosting. "Caffeine gives them the jitters."

She asked me to decorate the cakes. I took my time, squeezing red letters from a frosting tube. I wrote *G-R-O-V-E-R* on the big one. Crammed the little one with stars. I even made a squiggly sheep with a pink smile in honor of Lambie Pie. These days Grover carted that toy everywhere.

Kate pointed to my frosting lamb. "It looks like a cloud with legs."

I ignored her and made a teeny squiggle for the tail. I decorated till the tube was empty, then added a lollipop. Yellow. Grover's favorite color. I made that little cake fancy as Christmas. And Grover loved it. No sooner had we sung-screeched the last note of "Happy Good-bye, Dear Grover," than the kid did a nosedive and surfaced, grinning, stars smeared on his face. He even shared with Lambie Pie. A big goopy fistful of cake right in the lamb's little mouth.

Grover treated his presents like the cake. Bows were snatched and thrown, wrapping paper torn. "El," he said to the yellow ribbon from the twins, a new one for Lambie Pie. "Pan," he said to the overalls and card from the Torgles. "Beh! Beh! Beh!" He thumped my gift, his own copy of *Hop on Pop*.

That night before going to sleep, I carefully lined up Saint Jake Jock's trophy guys. The big batter, then the pitcher, all the way down to the smallest football player. Twelve of them on the shelf, picking up a blue shine from my night-light. They reminded me of the heavenly host supposedly up high with the stars. I'd heard about them from a few of my foster families who were big on going to church. I remembered those long, stiff-backed Sundays, full of thee-and-thou prayers. Whenever I tried to mumble along, here came a word like *trespass* or *tribulation* to trip up my tongue. Mostly I sat silent.

Sitting on Jake's bed, I gazed up at the trophies. I imagined Mr. T. tossing a ball to baby Jake, taking him to Little League, cheering for him in high school. I thought of Jake, safe and smiling. Grover should have that, too. And if a few *thee*s and *thou*s would help, well, I'd wrap my tongue around them. I ran a few prayers through my mind but none matched the kid's situation. So I bowed my head and said straight out, "Look, not to tell you how to do your job, but please don't forget Grover. He might need some help with that mother of his."

I didn't send my words to any spirit in particular. Maybe whoever heard would help.

Beyond the window a few stars blinked. Never could see those first gleams without thinking of Gram. The sight always gave me a little pick-me-up, to use some of her favorite words.

Who knew what might happen the next day? Tracey might change her mind. She might disappear again. Then Grover could still live with the Torgles. He could still live with me.

Tracey and Jenny were due to arrive at nine-thirty. That morning Grover was fed, washed, and packed to go by nine o'clock.

Five minutes later he started fussing. "La," he whimpered, but soon worked up to a holler. "La!"

He wanted Lambie Pie.

We looked at one another. No one knew where it was.

Kate wiggled a teddy bear in his face, but he shoved it away.

"La! La! La!" he cried.

Mr. T. and I organized a full-scale search. We dug through Grover's boxes and bags. Kate searched the bedroom and Jango the kitchen. Mrs. T. sang "Itsy-bitsy Spider" and Charmaine barked.

The kid screeched louder: "La! La! La!"

Finally I found the toy inside the bathtub. Even with a new yellow ribbon, Lambie Pie looked more like Myron the Chihuahua than a cuddly sheep. But Grover grabbed the poor thing and gave it two kisses.

And he gave me a big kiss, too.

Boom, there went that feel-good spotlight inside my chest. I didn't even mind the apple juice he spilled down my shirt.

That's when a car bumped up the drive in clouds of August dust. Fifteen minutes late.

When Tracey and Jenny stepped out, Mr. T. offered coffee and leftover good-bye cake. Tracey said no. She wanted to load up Grover's stuff and get him settled at home. She said this twice, practically licking her lips, like "home" was something Grover would find delicious.

"We bought you a crib and bureau." Tracey hunkered down beside Grover, who was clutching Lambie Pie and sucking his thumb. "They're secondhand but in really good shape." Tracey smiled at us all, even me. "I stenciled trucks on the walls of his room," she continued. "Pictures are supposed to be stimulating."

I wanted to roll my eyes. Tracey *still* didn't know much about Grover. The kid liked pictures of animals; he got bored with machines.

"I didn't finish the stencils till this morning—that's why we're late." Tracey glanced at Jenny, then rubbed a chipped blue moon on her fingernail. "I ran out of black paint, so one wheel is green."

"I'm sure Grover will like green," said Mrs. T.

"No, he won't," Jango broke in. "His favorite color is yellow. That's what Ben says."

Grover's thumb popped out of his mouth. "El," the kid said.

The silence that followed was broken by Mr. T.'s "ahhh." He turned to Jenny. "How's work going? You work for some doctors, right?"

"I'm a medical receptionist," Jenny said quickly, as if trying to help him end the silence. "The docs are pretty good about my schedule so I can take classes at night."

Medical—that's good, I thought. Jenny probably knew about Dr. Spock.

Then another thought hit me: If Jenny was working during the day and going to college at night, Grover would spend most of his time with Tracey. Who knew what could happen? That girl was so careless—

"School going well?" Mr. T.'s question broke into my thoughts.

"Yes, yes," said Jenny. "Thank you."

Silence again.

"I can repaint the wheel," Tracey said. All the excitement seemed to have seeped out of her.

Jenny gave her sister's shoulder a gentle squeeze. "I think it's time to go," she said.

The twins and I helped load the car. Boxes of clothes. Bags of toys and books. Everything I owned could fit inside one suitcase with six locked pockets. How had a guy as young as Grover managed to get so much stuff? And that wasn't counting the crib, changing table, and high chair. They would stay behind for the next foster baby.

I was double-checking Grover's room, opening one drawer—empty—after another—empty, empty—when I felt someone behind me.

"We're ready," came Jenny's voice.

I kept my face turned away. DON'T come in. I silently willed. DON'T ask questions.

I squeezed my eyes shut. DON'T take Grover.

When I opened my eyes, I spotted a rubber band on the floor. I picked it up, snapped it once. Stuck it in my pocket.

After today I wouldn't have to worry about the human vacuum cleaner. I wouldn't have to search out things before they could hurt him.

Jenny cleared her throat. "You'll have to visit us soon, Ben. Hey, Eileen told me you were the master chef when she hurt her back. Maybe you can make us your specialty. I love pancakes."

Kate yelled from downstairs: "Tracey says it's time to go."

Time to go.

I didn't move. I wanted to stretch time way out, like a rubber band. I wanted to keep it from moving on. I searched my brain for something to cause a delay. All I could come up with was a question. "Um"—I curled my fingers round the rubber band in my pocket—"what does the *G* stand for?"

"The *G?*" Jenny sounded confused.

"In Grover G. Graham."

"Oh." Jenny half laughed, half sighed. "It doesn't stand for anything. Tracey thought Grover G. Graham sounded distinguished. She said three *G*s meant three times as great."

Stupid, stupid, stupid. What mother saddles a kid with a meaningless name? A name screaming "Look at me!" Didn't Tracey know it was better, safer, to blend in?

Jenny continued, "And she got 'Grover' from *Sesame Street*."

Poor kid. Named for a fuzzy blue puppet. Thank God Sarah Jewel hadn't done that to me. Or maybe Gram had named me. Maybe Sarah Jewel had been happy to let someone—anyone—fill in my birth certificate.

"Tracey gets an idea or wants something—*boom!*—she acts." Jenny laugh-sighed again. "She accuses me of being too careful."

"You and Jenny," Tracey had said. *"Two old bats, squeaky and scared."*

"She's so excited Grover is coming home," said Jenny. "I thought she'd stencil the whole apartment."

I thought about the little guy downstairs, holding tight to his scrawny stuffed lamb. The system was full of kids whose parents wanted them one minute—and didn't the next. What if Tracey treated Grover like that? What if she wasn't there when he needed her? What if he cried and she didn't bother to come?

I asked Jenny to wait and disappeared into Jake's room.

I wasn't gone long. And when I placed the object in her palm, I didn't glance at it, not even once. "The first night in a new place—it can be scary," I explained. "If Grover wakes up and sees the blue glow, I think he'll be okay."

Jenny traced the plastic edge of my night-light. Then she started talking real low. Not really to me, though. More like she was working something out for herself. "When Grover was born, I should have taken a semester off," she said. "His father had already disappeared."

"But you needed to finish—"

"That's what I told myself." Jenny frowned down at the

night-light. "But really I was furious at Tracey. Skipping school. Getting pregnant. I was already trying to support us both—and then a baby." She passed the night-light from one hand to the other. "I didn't help as much as I should have. . . ." She looked at me. "Remember I said stubborn can make you tough or hard?"

I nodded.

"I was hard."

"Ben, Jenny," Mrs. T. called up the stairs. "The car's all packed."

Time to go.

Outside, Grover was squeezing Lambie Pie. He stared at the faces around him: Tracey; Jenny; his social worker, who had arrived when we were upstairs and who would make sure the return went smoothly. I could see the little guy tighten his grip on his lamb.

Mr. T. put the car seat in Jenny's car and strapped Grover in. The kid was kissed by everyone. Then the social worker's car pulled out, followed by Jenny's. I watched as it moved down the driveway. I saw Grover's Tweety Bird head at the window. Even with a stranglehold on that lamb, he was flapping and flapping his fist.

Bye-bye.

Beside me, Jango chewed on her Barbie.

Kate started to cry.

Mr. and Mrs. T. shaded their eyes and waved.

When the car had disappeared, Kate hiccuped once and rubbed her eyes. We all went inside. Everything was quiet. Charmaine licked a few Cheerios from the floor. Mrs. T. cut loose the balloon, now saggy, from Grover's high chair.

She gave it to the twins. I could hear the *snip-snip* of their scissors as I trudged upstairs. Making rubber dresses for their dolls.

In Jake's room, the trophies were lined up, neat as last night. I curled up on the bed. Stayed there for a while.

Chapter Seventeen

I woke up several times that night. Searched for the blue glow and remembered. Finally I turned on the hall light and left my door slightly open. Watching that bit of brightness, I fell asleep.

The sun was polishing the trophy guys when I opened my eyes the next morning. I heard the screen door slam. Then Kate started squealing, loud and long, making noise enough for four sets of twins.

I didn't even waste time wondering why. I had my own thoughts to figure through. *You'll have to visit,* Jenny had said.

"Why not today?" I said right out loud.

I tugged on a T-shirt. Yellow. Grover's favorite color. Hey, maybe things weren't so bad. At least the little guy hadn't moved far away. I could still see him. Maybe I could visit a few times a week, as Tracey had done.

But when I seated myself at the table, ready to announce

my plan, Kate was clutching a card covered with bluebirds. She read the note written inside: " 'Dear Kate the Great and my pretty Jingo-Jango Bell. Here's a little something for that first day of school. Be good. I love you and miss you. Dad.' "

Kate grinned and waved two twenty-dollar bills. "Here's the 'little something.' " Then she read the message all over again.

I listened to every word. Dear old Dad hadn't written a thing about returning or visiting or even taking three minutes to call and say boo. But the way Kate was carrying on, you'd think the man had stamped and mailed himself.

It was pitiful.

Apparently Jango thought so, too. All during Kate's grinning and waving and singsong reading, the girl had sat straight in her chair, smoothing her Barbie's yellow balloon dress. Finally she muttered, "Did he say when he was coming back?"

"Soon, I bet!" Kate ran the bills through her fingers. "*Forty* dollars, Jango! We can buy those pens that write in three colors. And new notebooks. Pink. And—"

Jango lifted the card from Kate's hand and silently read the message.

"My name"—her eyes never looked up from the card— "is Lenora."

"Hey, Jango!" Kate tossed the twenties like two pieces of confetti. "Maybe we can buy those shoes in—"

"Lenora."

The bills drifted to the table while Kate stared at her twin. "Lenora?" She wrinkled her nose. "But at school you wanted everybody to call you Jango, remember? It was the name Daddy—"

"I hate that name," Jango said in a little, hard voice.

Kate picked up the bills. "Jango," she said.

"Lenora."

I could tell this name thing could go on all morning. I'd have to step in. Tracey might decide to take Grover shopping or something. If we stopped by, they would be gone.

"Mrs. T.," I said. "Mrs. T."

She was watching Jango. "What, Ben?"

I took a deep breath, "Let's visit Grover today."

Mrs. T. brought her eyes to me, then glanced at Mr. T. "I think," she said, "we better let Grover settle in first."

Settle in? How long did it take to settle in? The kid had already been gone for one whole day.

Mrs. T. put down her coffee cup. "I know you miss Grover, Ben," she said. "We all do. But he needs—"

"Jingo Jango," said Kate.

"—to get used to living with his mother. Kate, quiet!" Mrs. T. thumped the table. "It's best to give Grover and Tracey a chance to . . . adjust. In a few weeks, maybe we can all stop by."

A few weeks? That would be September.

"But who will check on Grover?" I cried.

Mrs. T. took my hand. "Grover will be okay. Tracey will take care of him."

"But Jenny said I should visit *soon*." The words burst from me.

"I think she meant in a few weeks."

"Soon is *not* a few weeks." I shook off Mrs. T.'s hand.

"Ben, listen—"

"Jingo Jango," yelled Kate.

Rrriipp. Jango suddenly tore the bluebird card in half.

Rrriipp. She tore it again. And again. Then she snatched up her Barbie and ran from the table. Bits of card fluttered behind her.

Kate burst into tears.

"Jango!" Mrs. T. jumped up. "Oh, the poor—"

"Eileen." Mr. T. spoke. "Let her be."

"But she's so upset!"

"Of course she is." Mr. T. rose from his chair and began gathering the pieces of card. "She needs to be with herself for a bit—and then maybe she'll want to talk."

"You think so? Yes, you're right." Mrs. T. sighed and turned her attention to Kate.

I watched Mr. T. pick up a scrap. I listened to Kate's sobs and Mrs. T.'s murmurs, but the sounds seemed far away. I didn't move from my chair. September, I kept thinking. I might be at my next foster home by then. I might not even be here.

Mr. T. held the scraps in his cupped hands. "Ben, I think I need an assistant."

I wished I could just run off like Jango, but Mr. T. was already moving toward the stairs, so I managed to get my legs moving in a slow walk.

September, September, September: the word repeated in my head as I followed the man to the biggest bedroom. The desk there was as cluttered as the hardware store where he worked. Paper everywhere. Plus pens, pencils, a few safety pins. A bowl of paper clips was perched on the black phone. Through the window I could see Jango sitting under the sweetgum tree. I watched Charmaine bound up and flop down beside a yellow spot—Barbie's balloon dress—on the grass.

"That dog," I snorted, "is always hungry for a pat."

"It works out pretty well, don't you think?" Mr. T. re-arranged some papers and pens, clearing off a spot on the desk. "Charmaine wants to take what Jango wants to give. I'd call that taking a kind of giving."

Under the sweetgum, Jango was stroking Charmaine's head while the dog gently panted. What was Mr. T. talking about? Charmaine was just being her usual greedy self.

I watched the man place five scraps on the desk. He glanced at the others in his hand, chose one, and set it beside a blue piece.

Then it hit me. Mr. T. was actually going to *fix* the card. All the things in the house and yard that needed patching and *this* was what he chose.

He taped a teeny claw to a bit of bird foot.

"Money and a stupid card," I said after a while. "Like that would make up for not calling all summer. It's pitiful."

Mr. T. agreed. He connected a beak to a scrap of blue.

"Then why are you fixing *his* card?"

"I suppose"—Mr. T. pushed three small pieces together—"it's the one thing I *can* fix for Jango." He tapped a scrap. "Tell me, Ben. Would you call that an eye?"

I bent closer, then shook my head. "It's part of a letter," I said. "See how the black line curves?"

"How about that." Mr. T. pushed a few pieces my way. "What do you make of these?"

We puzzled for a while in silence. I swear I was going cross-eyed from staring at all those bitty bits of blue, black, and white. "Fixing this card is a waste of time." I tossed down the tape. "Jango doesn't want it. She'll just tear it up again."

"Ahhh." Mr. T. turned two scraps this way and that. "It

106

might sound strange, but I've seen it happen. Some folks will destroy what they want the most."

Some folks will destroy what they want the most. Mr. T. was making *no* sense today. Jango didn't want the card, so she had torn it up. Simple as that. I'd do the same. If I got a card from the Crawdiches or the DeBernards or the Hartmans . . . if I got a card from Sarah Jewel Watson, I'd tear it right up. In a heartbeat. I wouldn't take one pitiful thing they tried to give me.

I thought about Jango and that card. Maybe she had destroyed it because she *did* want it. Or maybe what she *really* wanted was her dad. It was confusing. Maybe she wanted her dad so much it hurt less to shut him out. I glanced out the window. The girl was still under the sweetgum, patting Charmaine.

"I think we should go outside," I said.

"Good idea." Mr. T. held up the card. "Ta-da. Almost as good as new."

I don't know why he was ta-da-ing so proudly. That card was chaos with a capital *C*. It was thick with tape and chockful of crooked letters and birds.

Mr. T. grinned. "Well, at least it's in one piece rather than fifty," he said, opening a small drawer in the desk.

He drew out something silver and slim and touched his thumb to a button.

Click. A circle of light played on my wrist.

Mr. T. closed my fingers over the flashlight. "I always found this helpful on dark nights," he said.

Did he know why I'd kept the hall light on the night before? Did he know about my night-light? I stiffened. If he was going to start asking questions about Grover, he'd find himself putting that flashlight back in the drawer, thank you very much. If he was going to scratch at my feelings, like Ms. Burkell, he'd soon be talking to empty air.

I felt the flashlight's cool weight in my fist. I could see Mr. T.'s big red hand over mine and all the little hairs on his wrist. I thought of that hand taping up Jango's card. I thought of it patting Grover's back. Gently it tapped my knuckles.

I looked up. All the lines in Mr. T.'s face were creating a smile. "It's a present, Ben. It won't bite."

I had to smile back. I didn't have much experience with surprise presents—just the suitcase from Myron the Chihuahua—but I thought of what Mr. T. had said before. How taking could be a kind of giving.

"Okay." I allowed my hand to tighten on the flashlight. "I mean, thanks."

As I followed Mr. T. downstairs I slipped the flashlight into my pocket. I could feel it there, bumping my hip. I decided I'd lock it in my suitcase. Or maybe I'd push aside a few trophy guys and make space for it on the shelf. Something shiny of mine beside all Jake's gold.

When Kate saw us, she leaped up the stairs. "You fixed it!" she yelled, grabbing for the card.

"Hold up a minute, Miss Kate." Mr. T. tousled her hair. "Ben's going to let your sister have the first look."

"But Jango will just tear it up," Kate cried.

"Then we'll have to fix it again."

Lord, I hope not, I thought as I made my way to the sweetgum. I ran my finger over the card. That tape was thick as a scar. I sure didn't relish sticking it all over again to fifty pieces of beak and bird feet and cloud.

I found Jango braiding Charmaine's hair and poking gumballs on the clumps. That dog was holding herself straight and still, just like a lady at the beauty shop.

"Hey, Jango," I said.

She didn't look up. She didn't stop braiding.

I held out the card. "It's fixed," I said.

She continued to braid.

I felt stupid, just standing there. What was I supposed to do? Ms. Burkell would yammer about feelings. Mrs. T. would probably hug. Mr. T.? Mr. T. would say "Ahhh."

"Ahhh," I said, still holding the card straight out. "Listen, Jango—"

"Lenora," she snapped.

I blinked at her force. "Okay, whatever. Lenora."

She stuck a gumball on Charmaine. "What?"

I waved the card.

"Put it on the grass," she said, going back to braiding.

I carefully placed the card beside her Barbie. I guessed that was my signal to leave, but for some reason, I stayed. Jango, or Lenora or whatever she called herself, was frowning so fiercely, her eyebrows practically met above her nose. And the gumballs were piling up on Charmaine.

I hunkered down beside the Barbie. Since the poor thing wasn't being chomped on, I could get a good look at its feet. Nothing more than stumps. Pitiful.

I fished in my pocket and pulled out the flashlight, then dug deeper for the fuzz, popcorn kernels, and rubber bands

I'd picked up before Grover, the human vacuum cleaner, had moved out. Quickly I wrapped first one rubber band, then the other, around the Barbie stumps.

"Rubber shoes to match the rubber dress," I pointed out, feeling dumb. Those bitten-up feet seemed like such a teeny thing to try to fix. Jango's dad—now, that was who I'd really like to fix. And I bet Mr. T. would have a few words to say to him, too.

Jango reached out. She touched one of the rubber bands with the tip of her finger; then her face kind of crumpled.

Oh, Lord, I thought in a panic. She's going to cry. What should I do? Grover I could deal with, but a crying *girl* . . . I dug my hands deep in my pockets.

But Jango pulled herself together, sniffing hard. She traced the rubber-band shoes on her Barbie. "They look like old-time sandals," she finally said.

"Like the Romans wore." I nodded, then suggested awkwardly, "Maybe you can make your Barbie a toga or something. That's what a Roman dress is called."

Charmaine suddenly shook herself. The gumballs trembled in her fur.

I watched Jango stroke Charmaine's head. "You trying to turn that dog into a porcupine?" I asked. "What's with the gumballs?"

"Hair decorations." Jango smiled a little. "Like your social worker's."

I pictured Ms. Burkell's teeny braids and all those bouncy beads. I cast my eyes at Charmaine.

"I know, I know." Jango plucked a gumball from the dog's back. "It's not quite the same look."

I untangled a gumball. Jango began unbraiding the dog.

We worked together in silence, while Charmaine gently panted.

"Pitiful," I said loudly. The word just popped out. I guessed I was referring to the taped-up card, the Barbie shoes, Charmaine's hairdo. All three. Maybe her dad, too.

Jango didn't answer. Probably trying to blank it all out.

When she finally spoke, her voice was low. "Dad cried all the time, when Mom died. He didn't go to work. Sometimes he didn't get out of bed."

Jango pressed a gumball into her palm. "I thought Dad would die, too," she said softly. "And then when the crying stopped"—she took a deep breath—"he said he would find a better job. He said we would have stuff again—dresses and pink things, like when Mom was alive—and then—"

"He left."

Jango poked the gumball back on Charmaine. "He needed to get away." Now her voice was very low. "We slowed him down. We cost money."

"But he hasn't even called."

"Maybe he thinks"—Jango pulled the gumball out—"the crying will start all over again."

"What kind of stupid reason . . . ?" I was almost yelling; then I noticed her shoulders, all hunched. I thought of all the excuses I'd made for Sarah Jewel: She was young. She had to get away. I'd slow her down.

I gently removed the gumball Jango was twisting into Charmaine's fur.

"He won't come back." Jango ran her fingers through a tangled braid. "No matter what Kate says."

111

I didn't know what to say that wouldn't be a lie. "You know, Jango," I said after a minute, "my mother never came back."

"I know," she replied, looking straight at me. "And remember, my name is Lenora."

Chapter Eighteen

For the rest of the day Kate tried every trick—bossing, begging, pouting—to get Lenora to change back to Jango. It wasn't going to happen. Lenora was now Lenora. Kate even wanted me to help tease her twin, but I flat-out refused. And that bossy girl tried to kick me.

Even in the midst of dodging Kate, I couldn't shake off my talk with Lenora. I kept thinking about the twins' dad. The man had practically disappeared from their lives. And Sarah Jewel—she could still be riding Greyhound buses, for all I knew. Mother, father—you just couldn't count on them. One minute you could be walking with them on a nailed-down rug; the next minute—*boom!*—they pull it out from under you. You're left flat on your back, feet waving, confused as a tipped-over turtle.

Well, I wouldn't let that happen to Grover. Mrs. T. could fill my ears with talk of Tracey's changed ways, Kate could praise her. The system could say the girl was "fit" to take care of her baby. Lord knows the system makes mistakes.

When Ms. Burkell called that afternoon, I cut in on her cheery "hello."

"How does the system decide who is fit?" I asked.

I heard her startled breathing.

I kept on going. "What gets looked at? Is there a list? You gotta look at more than the surface, you know."

"What do you mean?"

I went on. "In one house I had my own bathroom. Peach-colored towels and soaps shaped like shells. Nice, huh?"

"Go on."

"But the shower faucet didn't work right. And the mat was a killer. The first time I stepped on that mat, it slid."

I took a breath. "I fell and the hot water kept pouring down. I had to crawl out of the tub."

"Ben—"

"And sheets," I said.

"Sheets?"

"Yes, sheets. How often do they get washed? One place didn't wash them the whole time I was there. Six months. That can't be good for a baby. You need three to six sheets, that's what Dr. Spock—"

"Dr. Spock?"

I gripped the phone. "I just want to know if those things get checked," I said. "Faucets and sheets. They should get checked, you know, before a home is considered fit."

I hurried on. "And food. Sometimes people skip meals—"

"Ben, what's wrong?" Ms. Burkell sounded worried. "Do you have enough to eat?"

I leaned my head against the wall. This wasn't about me, but I didn't want to tell her about Grover. I didn't want anyone asking questions. A nosey grown-up could make everything worse.

"Do you want to go somewhere and talk?" Ms. Burkell asked.

"I'm okay."

The woman hesitated. "Actually, I was calling with some news," she went on. "There's a good chance you'll be settled with a new family before school starts. Closer to downtown Greenfield. I know you were hoping for that."

Grover's high chair ready for the next baby. Jake's room for the next stray.

"Ben?"

I pictured the bounce-bounce of her forever cheery beads. That was right. Time to move on. I was temporary.

"The Torgles told me you and the little boy really hit it off."

"Grover." My throat was tight, but I got the word out. "His name is Grover."

"How do you feel—"

"I have to go," I said, and hung up.

Don't you know, Ms. Burkell called back the next afternoon. Some social workers might not check a stray for months. It was my luck to get a nosey one.

"I wanted to see if you were okay."

"I'm okay."

"If you ever want to talk . . ."

Yeah, sure. I wondered if Ms. Burkell would bring up

Sarah Jewel again. DON'T, I thought. DON'T mention her name. I hadn't thought about this person for ages, and then Ms. Burkell had to go and plant thoughts of her in my head. Well, I didn't want any stories about permanent homes. I didn't want any fairy god-awful mother flitting in and out of my life. Look at Tracey. Whisking Grover off to some happily-ever-after home. With Jenny gone most of the time, who would check the faucets and sheets? Who would make sure Grover got his meals? Who would check to see if he was scared of the dark or locked in a time-out closet or hit till the bruises came?

"Ben?"

"I have to go," I said, and hung up.

After I replaced the phone, I stood there for a minute. Mrs. T. had said we wouldn't visit Grover for a few weeks, but she hadn't said anything about calling. One phone call, that was all I wanted. And I would make that call myself, thank you very much. If I asked Mrs. T., she would just tell me Grover was fine.

To make a call, though, I needed Tracey's number. The Torgles must have written it down somewhere. In my mind, I made a list of likely places.

A. The pile of papers by the kitchen phone

B. The pile of papers on the table by the front door

C. Somewhere on the Torgles' desk in their bedroom

Over the next two days, I checked out A and B. What a mess. Receipts, empty envelopes, scraps of paper marked with a few words. I read every bit of handwriting. Actually, I told myself, it was more like I was cleaning than searching. In fact, when Mr. T. wanted to know what I was doing, I asked if he had ever heard of a modern invention called the trash can. A lame joke. But he grinned and handed me one.

Checking out C was harder. I had to stay behind while the Torgles took the twins to the rec center pool. The girls were still wrestling over names. Even though Kate no longer chanted "Jango," the word *Lenora* never passed her lips. I guess Kate was having trouble losing the name. After all, His Royal Wonderfulness, their father, had given it to her twin. Myself, I used the name Lenora whenever I could. "Lenora, pass the peas." "Lenora, is it raining?" I figured the girl needed someone cheering her on. She wasn't even chewing her Barbie anymore, just carrying it around by the hair. If she wanted to be called Zippity Moon Pie, that was what I would call her.

"Zippity Moon Pie," I murmured, trying to calm myself as I pushed open the Torgles' bedroom door. My heart was ramming my chest. Here I was, being sneaky, just as Tracey had said. Well, I was doing this for Grover.

I almost had a heart attack when Charmaine brushed by.

"Out," I said, pointing to the door.

Charmaine flopped down at my feet.

I kept my eyes focused on the desk. Fixed on the black phone, paper clips, and piles of paper. I didn't let myself even glance at the rest of the room. That kind of looking seemed sneakier than searching. It was snooping.

I shuffled, lifted, read every bit of paper and carefully put it back. Charmaine suddenly yawned and—*ta-dum*—

my heart punched my chest. I took a deep breath. I pushed back my mind-picture of Mr. T. piecing together that ripped-up card. Of him handing me the flashlight, tapping my knuckles. I wasn't *taking* anything. I wasn't even snooping. I was just *looking*.

I found a book labeled Addresses but—wouldn't you know—there was no listing under *G* for Graham and it was stuffed with as many papers as the desk. *Finally* I found the scrap, brown and wrinkled, I was searching for. I copied Tracey's phone number and, just in case, her address. The Wilkshire, 821 Decatur Street, apartment 402.

I knew the Wilkshire. The apartment building was a few blocks from the library.

Charmaine thumped her tail and I almost dropped the address book. I quickly put it back. The Torgles would never know I was here. Maybe being sneaky was the best way to deal. What's the use of asking questions? Blabbing? Boo-hooing? Never changed a thing.

I checked out the window. The yellow brown yard looked flat-out beat by the sun. No sign yet of the Torgle-mobile.

I picked up the black phone. Dialed a number.

One ring.

Two.

Three. Four. Five.

"Hello." Tracey's voice. "Hello?"

If Tracey knew I was calling, she'd hang right up. Barely breathing, I gripped the phone, listening hard for Grover sounds.

Rattle-jiggle-cough. Charmaine's ears pricked and she raced out the door.

"Hello?"

I couldn't hear anything in the background. Where was Grover? Napping? Eating? Locked in a closet?

"Who *is* this?"

I heard the Torglemobile pull up outside. Charmaine barked. Doors slammed.

I quickly hung up. I wouldn't learn a thing about Grover from a phone call. I'd have to figure another way.

Chapter Nineteen

The twins' day at the pool had given them summer colds, which kept them home from the next trip downtown. On Saturday afternoon, it was just me and Mr. T. gunning the Torglemobile. The man did his ATM transaction in the usual way, pocketing half the money, winking, stashing the rest in the glove compartment. Drizzle drearied the air, matching my mood, turning Greenfield into Grayfield. I didn't feel much like listening to the worried talk between Mr. T. and the hardware-store clerk. And I sure didn't want to watch them watching the door, waiting for customers. I asked if I could stay at the library for a few hours. Mr. T. parked the car in the lot, said he'd meet me around five, and promised an Uddleston's milk shake. I watched as he lurched down the street.

Then I turned in my own direction. Not the library. I

took a right at the next street. I was looking for the Wilkshire on Decatur Street. Apartment 402.

You'll have to visit, Jenny had said the day Tracey took Grover.

That's what I planned to do.

As I walked the few blocks the drizzle tapered off and a few rays slid through the muggy gray. The sidewalk steamed. I wondered what new words Grover was spouting. What things he was dropping. If he would remember me.

I figured I'd sneak a quick peek at his crib sheets to judge their cleanness. I'd check the hot-water faucet and bath mat. I'd check the food supply. I'd check the nightlight. I figured I could do all that without Tracey catching on.

But would Tracey even let me in? I remembered her sneer: *You been raised by a perfect mama?* I remembered our face-off at the whirl-go-round.

How should I handle her?

To give myself time to plan, I circled to the back of the brick apartment building.

That's when I saw him.

Sucking his thumb. Rubbing Lambie Pie's ear.

Alone.

"Hey," I said softly. "Grover."

The kid snapped to, alert. He looked right . . . left . . . up.

"Grover!" At the unlocked gate, I waved like a fool. "Over here."

That's when he saw me. "Beh! Beh!" Grover grinned this almighty big grin. He gripped Lambie Pie's neck, wobbled to his feet, and plowed through the scrubby grass.

I could feel my own smile, big as his, when I hauled him into my arms.

"Beh! Beh!"

Jeesh, the kid was a mess. Dirt streaked his face and bare legs and dusted his sweaty curls. His diaper sagged practically down to the knees gripping my side. No telling how long he'd been wet.

And alone.

Just wait till Tracey Graham lollygagged her lazy self outside, I fumed, trying to keep Grover's grimy fingers out of his mouth. "Suck your thumb," I advised. "You've already cleaned the dirt off of it."

I scanned the brick face of the apartment building. Every window was blank. Tracey was probably inside. Reading a magazine. Gabbing on the phone. Watching TV.

I hauled up the little guy's diaper, smoothed back his hair, and tucked Lambie Pie under one arm. I prepared to march us into that building, up those stairs.

You'll have to visit, Jenny Graham had said.

I'd be visiting, all right.

Didn't Tracey know what could happen to a baby? He could wander out of the yard, into the street. He could choke on a pebble or twig. He could bang his head. Some stranger could stride through the unlocked gate, lift Grover, and leave. And Tracey would never know.

I slowed my pace.

"Beh, Beh, Beh," sang Grover.

Tracey Graham needed a good scare. That might shake some mother sense into her.

Give Tracey a good scare. At first that was all I planned to do.

Chapter Twenty

With Grover in my arms, I turned away from the gate and continued down the sidewalk. The sweat on my upper lip tasted like melted salt. At any moment, I expected to hear Tracey's yell, running footsteps . . . feel a jerk on my arm. My back tensed.

One foot in front of the other, in front of the other, in front . . .

"Twee." Grover pointed his toy lamb at everything we passed. "Gas. Flub."

"Tree," I said automatically. "Grass. Flower."

I'd hang out at the library with Grover for an hour or so. Enough time to make Tracey worry. That would teach her a lesson.

But when I spied the Torglemobile in the lot, I had an even better idea. Grover and I would wait for Mr. T. I'd tell him how I had found Grover. We would march straight to Apartment 402.

How could Tracey be considered fit after what she had

124

done? Leaving a baby alone was worse, much worse, than dirty sheets. Surely the system would take Grover away from her now. Maybe he could live with the Torgles again.

But how long would he stay? The system was always spitting kids from one place to the next. Look at me. I'd be leaving the Torgles soon.

I hoisted Grover higher as I leaned against the car door and tried to figure what to do. Jeesh, the kid had grown heavy as a bull calf.

"Ca," he crowed, banging the window.

"Car," I said. "Remember this car? Old car. Blue car."

Car with a jiggly door.

Car with a broken lock. Mr. T. had never fixed it.

I wish I could say I planned the whole escape. That I was cool as the hero in *Where Eagles Dare*, the book I'd checked out from the library. I wish I could say I rescued Grover as neatly as the hero rescued the American general from the enemy's fortress.

But my mind had a hard time trying to order things A, B, C. My thoughts came mostly in spurts.

Get money.

Get money. Take Grover.

Get money. Take Grover. Leave.

Yeah, Grover might be returned to the Torgles. But what if Mr. T. lost his job? What if they had to move? Or stopped taking in strays? What if Grover became difficult? Grew into someone they didn't want?

What if Tracey got him again?

I opened the door, searched the glove compartment. I tucked the envelope into my pocket.

"No, no." I pried Grover's fingers from the dashboard.

"Time to go, little guy," I tried to say calmly. The money bulged in my pocket. I glanced around.

Grover's back arched in protest. His mouth opened.

"Ice cream," I said desperately. "Want some ice cream, Grover?"

"Keam!" Grover cried.

"Ice cream for Grover." I shut the car door and lugged him out of the parking lot.

"Keam!" Grover stuck out his tongue, licking an invisible cone.

"Soon," I promised, checking one end of the street for Mr. T., the other for Tracey.

"Keam!"

"Ice cream for big boy. Big cone for Grover," I sang. One foot in front of the other, in front of the other, in front . . .

"Keam, keam, keam," insisted Grover.

Believe me, the hero in *Where Eagles Dare* had it easy. Rescuing one reasonable, potty-trained general was a piece of cake compared to an ice cream—obsessed baby with a dirty diaper.

One foot in front of the other, in front, in front . . .

Get money. Take Grover. Leave.

Leave.

Leave.

As I walked signs grew larger. They hung in the air like huge, square balloons: Safeway. Uddleston's. Greyhound.

Leave.

Leave.

Greyhound bus.

Yeah.

Greyhound bus.

Okay, Grover would need things. Food. Diapers. Apple juice. I tried to remember baby stuff I had seen at the Torgles' house. Milk. I could buy little cartons when the bus stopped, so the milk wouldn't go bad.

At Safeway, I wrestled Grover and Lambie Pie into a metal cart. I remembered riding high in these carts a long time ago while Gram trundled behind. How did an old, old lady ever keep up with the busy baby I must have been? Maybe I was more mannerly than Grover, who was now snatching bags off the shelves.

"Cook," the kid cried, grabbing at a package of Oreos.

"Ap ju."

"Cheeze."

What a smart kid! Grover had learned a bunch of new words. I just wished he wouldn't say them so loudly. Or try to stand in the cart. Or shriek. People turned to look at us. Some smiled. Some didn't.

"Cute kid." The checkout clerk popped her gum. "Your brother?"

I started to shake my head but stopped. "Yes," I said softly. "We're brothers." The lie made me feel nervous—and proud. My brother, I thought, handing the clerk a bill from the envelope. Mr. T.'s envelope. I quickly shoved it back in my pocket.

"My little brother. Grover." I said the words nice and loud.

"Sure is a handful."

"Yeah." I sighed. That fast, Grover had bitten the plastic wrapping off a red lollipop. I fished it from his mouth, then wiped his lollipop spit on my shorts. I slapped down a few extra coins.

By the time Grover and I had staggered out of Safeway and into the bus station, red lollipop spit smeared the kid's chin and T-shirt, my chin and T-shirt, Lambie Pie, and the plastic grocery bag I'd slung over my shoulder.

"Someone enjoyed his candy." A gray-haired woman smiled at Grover, who flashed her a sticky grin.

That's when I realized the biggest hazard to Grover's rescue was Grover himself. See, a successful escape depends on blending in. I was aces at that—but Grover attracted smiles and waves wherever he went.

"Oh, the darling!" the woman cooed. "How old is he?"

"Almost seventeen months," I mumbled.

The woman patted the orange seat next to her. "Sit here," she offered. "Where are you boys going?"

Where *were* we going?

"Bye-bye." Grover waved his fist.

"You're going bye-bye!" The woman laughed. "What a clever boy."

"La!" Grover held out Lambie Pie for a kiss.

"I've got to change his diaper, ma'am," I interrupted, hauling the kid to the men's room. "Bye-bye," Grover called the whole way. "Bye-bye. Bye-bye."

I changed him at the sink, washed his face and hands, rubbed a wet paper towel over his hair. I dabbed at the lollipop stains on Lambie Pie, which only smeared them worse.

I stuck a few paper towels in the Safeway bag. I'd probably need them later.

Luckily when we sidled out of the men's room, the friendly lady had disappeared. She'd boarded a bus or been picked up, I guessed. I studied the list of towns and departure times posted on the wall. I figured the best plan would be to keep moving, buying tickets as we went, so we couldn't be as easily tracked. Maybe we could keep going till we reached Wyoming. Big sky, lots of land. Or New York City, with its bright lights and hordes of people. We could lose ourselves in the crowd.

Then Grover remembered I owed him an ice cream.

"Keam," he demanded. "Keam!"

"Okay." I hauled him to the counter. "Let's buy our tickets first."

"Keam!" Grover howled.

"Where you boys headed?" asked the man behind the counter.

"Richmond," I said, shoving bills in his direction.

The man winked at Grover. "If he's under two, he can ride for free, so long as he sits on your lap."

I glanced down at Grover. He was squinching his eyes, trying to wink back. He was also squirming and flailing his arms. I decided to take two tickets. There was no guarantee he'd stay on my lap.

The man counted the money and slowly wrote the tickets. "Brother?" He nodded toward Grover.

"Yeah." That glow of pride again.

"He don't favor you much."

I shrugged.

The man leaned his elbows on the counter, winked again at Grover.

"It's the same with me and my brother," he said, patting his round tummy. "Would you believe, to look at me, that my brother was a basketball star?"

"Yeah?"

The man nodded. "His senior year of high school, the team went all the way to state."

"Yeah?" I repeated, inching away from the counter. This guy was chattier than the old lady.

"You'd think with a brother like that at least I could make a free throw—but, no. And look at you two." The man tweaked Grover's nose. "I would never have guessed you were brothers. Not in a million years." He smiled. "But then, there's no predicting genes. What takes you boys to Richmond?"

This guy could go on and on and *on*. Didn't anyone else need a ticket?

"Um, we're visiting my—our—grandmother," I replied.

"Any bags to check?"

I shook my head. Wait, maybe we *should* have a bag. Most folks did. Would he suspect? I pictured my suitcase at the Torgles'.

"She . . . my grandmother has clothes for us at her house," I said. "We go there a lot."

Don't ramble. Slow down, I thought.

"Parents divorced?" The man tsk-tsked sympathetically. "We see a lot of kids traveling by themselves. Sad situation."

"Yeah," I agreed, glancing over my shoulder.

He perked up. "I've got family in Richmond. What's your grandmother's name?"

I glanced wildly at the counter, at the tickets, pens, clips—

"Staple," I said.

"Staple. Staple," the man mused. "Doesn't ring any bells. What part of Richmond she live in?"

Just then Grover, thank God, with precision timing, set up a howl for ice cream.

"I better get him some." I patted the kid's back. "Say bye-bye, big boy."

"Keam," yelled Grover.

"The three-fifteen bus to Richmond"—the man bye-byed with both hands—"leaves in ten minutes."

No time for ice cream. I hurried to the vending machine. Mints. Cookies. Chocolate bars. What kind of food was that for a little kid? Finally I slid in my quarters, pulled the knob under the Cheese Nips, and palmed a packet of crackers. They were as orange as the bus station seats, but at least the cheese part sounded healthy.

"Departing gate five," a voice squawked over the intercom. "Bus leaving for"—I listened hard to the garbled list of cities—"(something) . . . (something) . . . Richmond."

This was it. I adjusted the plastic Safeway bag, hoisted Grover high, and handed the driver our tickets. This close, I could see the summer sun silvering the bus. Up, up, up, I climbed the steps into the cool aisle and, knees a bit shaky, plopped Grover into an empty seat and took the one beside him.

"La!" Grover cried, scratching the plush covers.

"Yeah," I said, getting him settled. "I guess the seat does feel like Lambie Pie."

As the bus pulled away, Grover waved bye-bye to the station, the waiting people, the Uddleston's ice cream sign.

Bye-bye, Greenfield, I thought. Grover and I were finding our way out of the system.

I was leaving Greenfield exactly like Sarah Jewel. Riding high in a plush seat. Listening to wheels skimming past Safeway, past the library. Skimming onto the highway.

I wondered if Sarah Jewel had dreamed for years about leaving Greenfield. The first time she left, had she followed an A-B-C plan? Or one day, sitting at Uddleston's and slurping a shake, had she caught the flash of a passing bus? And decided, quick as a snap, to go?

Riding high, had she felt like me? Proud and scared and free?

And when she left Greenfield the second time, when I was a baby and she left me behind, had Sarah Jewel taken the Greyhound bus? I had been under two; I could have ridden for free. I would have slept quietly on her lap.

I wondered how she felt then.

Chapter Twenty-one

"Ga!" Grover broke into my thoughts. The kid had fished a paper towel from the Safeway bag and was shredding it.

I traded him Lambie Pie for the paper towel and gathered up the shreds. Then I tried to calculate time. If the bus had left at 3:15, it was probably about 3:25 now.

Less than an hour had passed since I first saw Grover alone. I wondered how I was going to keep him quiet till the next town, let alone the next *five* towns, till we reached Richmond.

But as the bus wheels hummed over the highway Grover's mouth opened, his eyes closed, and he dozed off. You never knew with the kid. Once in a while, just by accident, he did exactly what you needed him to do.

I leaned my head against the plush seat and tried to figure what to do next. I wanted to think logically—A, B, C—but my mind boomeranged: D. X. P. Z.

Maybe I should check out our money situation, I finally

decided. How much did we have? How much did I owe Mr. T.? The Torgles could keep all my stuff. The foster-kid clothes weren't worth much, but the suitcase was practically new, with money in the second pocket. I had arrived with $129.37 and spent $8.35 on Grover's *Hop on Pop* present. That left $121.02. If I owed more, I would pay Mr. T. back when we got to where we were going. I'd get a job and mail him the cash.

I'd have to mail it from another town, though. I didn't want anyone checking the postmark, tracking us down.

Mr. T. could take back the flashlight he'd given me. He could find it easily. It stood, lens down, on Jake's trophy shelf.

My mind boomeranged some more: Q. D. K. E.

I could get a job. Slinging fries, delivering newspapers. I could tack on a few years to my age.

Tracey would probably be calling the police soon, if she hadn't already. Mr. T. would find me and the money gone. What would he think?

Outside, the rain had started again and the windshield wipers *shlip-shlipp*ed as Grover snuffled softly in sleep. Funny little guy. I wished I had a jacket or something to tuck over him.

But this was not the time for wishing. If the old woman and the ticket seller were any clue, we'd be fielding plenty of questions. Questions about where we were from, where we were going. I needed to come up with a good story—fast. Let's see, Grover and I were brothers, the Staples, traveling from Greenfield to Richmond to visit our grandmother, Maureen Staple. I would tell people that Grover was a year and a half and I was thirteen.

I counted the money: $153 in bills. Let's see, I had

shelled out $30 for the two tickets and $17.19 for supplies at Safeway. That meant I had stolen—borrowed—$200.

Two hundred dollars! The money weighed kind of heavy in my hand. Remembering the light-fingered Saint Stephen's boy, I slipped a few bills into each of the four pockets of my shorts. If one got picked, we wouldn't be completely broke. The Torgles would have enough for the week, I kept telling myself. Let's see, $200 minus the $121.02 in my suitcase pocket equals $78.98. I still owed the Torgles $78.98. I'd mail it as soon as I could.

Maybe Mr. and Mrs. T. would give my suitcase to the twins. The girls would like it, I bet. I remembered them playing with the locks and pockets when I first moved in.

That seemed like a long time ago.

I started to count the bills again, but before I had finished, the bus turned off the highway and came to a stop. Town Number One and a ten-minute rest stop.

Grover woke up instantly, demanding "ju." I popped the top on one of the apple juice cans, but of course, he wanted to hold it. Soon half the drink soaked his shirt and mine.

"It's okay, Grover." I mopped him with a paper towel while he squirmed and hollered, "Ow!"

Out. He wanted out.

But I didn't want to risk leaving the bus. What if we missed it? What if we met another too friendly soul? Someone with more questions than I had stories?

What if we ran into a police officer or security guard? Someone trained to spot kids on the run?

I handed Grover a Cheese Nip. He bit it hard and orange crumbs sprinkled the plush seat.

"Beh! Beh!" The kid offered me a soggy half.

I nibbled a bit, just to make him smile. Then the bus started again and Grover went back to gnawing his Nip. No telling how long his good mood would last, though. I wished I'd had the time to buy him a toy or book—but hey! I knew *Hop on Pop* by heart. So while day turned into night and shadows hunkered outside, while the wheels shooshed over the highway, I recited the entire book.

"Ba," commanded Grover.

I repeated the whole thing again. And again.

Then I caught the sound of a baby snore. When I kissed the top of his sleeping head, I smelled sweat, dirt, apple juice, lollipop.

Everything would be fine. I'd take care of the kid. I'd feed him real peanut butter crackers, not weird-colored Nips. Pancakes whenever he wanted. I'd fix him a whole yellow room full of stencils. Happy sheep and horses and high-flying birds, not stupid trucks with one green wheel. I'd protect him from every bad thing in the system. I'd never leave him behind.

I looked out the window, hoping for stars, but all I saw was rain.

My own eyelids were closing and I must have dozed off, because it seemed only minutes before the bus jerked to a stop, the lights came on, and we were at Town Number Two.

Grover continued to snooze, and I watched sleepily as a few passengers lollygagged off and on, munching potato chips, sipping Cokes. Rain slithered down the windows and drummed on the bus top, making the inside dim and cozy.

The driver swung into his seat, checked the rearview mirror, and gripped the steering wheel.

Then came a knock on the door.

The door opened, and first the cap, then the head, then the uniformed shoulders appeared as a policeman climbed the three steps onto the bus, bent, and spoke to the driver, who glanced back . . . nodded once.

The bus lights glared, folks shifted and grumbled and peered . . . then fell silent as those shoes, those shiny black shoes, began to step, step, step up the aisle.

Chapter Twenty-two

Grover snoozed on.

No way to run.

Nowhere to run.

I hunched down in the seat, barely breathing.

Step, step, step.

I could see the shoes coming. Shiny and black. Neatly tied laces.

Step, step, step.

Maybe—please, please, please—the man was after someone else. Stay low, stay quiet, don't panic. A, B, C.

A hand came down on my shoulder.

The policeman brought his face close to mine. There were raindrops on his lashes and cap. His face was smooth and thin and serious.

"What's your name, son?"

My heart pounded. "Ben Staple."

"And who is this?" The cap tilted in Grover's direction and a few drops slid to my lap.

"My brother."

"Your brother?"

"Yes."

"Well, Ben, I'm going to ask you and your brother to step off the bus for a moment. I need you to answer a few questions."

"Will it take long?"

"I hope not."

I licked my lips. "My grandmother will be worried. She's waiting for us."

"What's her name?"

"Maureen Staple," I said, then added louder: "Mrs. Maureen Staple of Richmond, Virginia."

"Give me her phone number," said the policeman. "I'll call and put her mind at ease."

"Her phone number?" My brain refused to work. It seemed to be stuck.

The cap nodded and rain showered softly. I couldn't look up from the teeny drops on my hands.

The policeman sighed and leaned over me. Lifted the sleeping baby.

Grover woke up then, eyes wide, staring up at the stranger. "Beh, Beh," he cried, turning, twisting to find me.

"Shhh," I whispered. Those shiny black shoes began to step, step, step to the front of the bus. I followed. All around, eyes and whispers. Eyes and whispers. "What?" "What happened?" "Those boys."

My insides felt full of broken glass. Like I was getting cut inside.

When we stepped out the door, the driver started the engine. Rain slanted into my eyes. I had to squint as I watched the bus slide, mist silver, into the darkness, grow smaller . . . smaller . . . disappear.

From far away I heard Grover's cries and wondered if I would be cuffed.

"Here, *please* take the little tyke." The policeman passed Grover to me. "He doesn't seem to like me."

Grover wrapped his arms and legs around me like a frightened monkey. I held my arm above his head, trying to shield him from the rain.

A large hand prodded my back, directing me to a squad car.

"La," Grover sniffled, rubbing his nose on Lambie Pie.

"McDevitt, what'd you do to that little boy?" An older policeman laughed behind the wheel. "I bet his screams carried clear to the station."

"Aw, shut up." McDevitt grinned. "Next time, *you* go out in the rain."

The one called McDevitt settled us in the backseat, shook himself like Charmaine, and climbed into the front.

He turned. "What's your name?"

Silence.

"Look, kid," McDevitt sighed. "You can make this hard or you can make it easy. Let's try again. Name?"

"Ben Watson," I whispered.

"And the baby?"

"Grover. Grover G. Graham."

"Big name for a little guy."

"It sounds distinguished," I said, "according to his mother."

"We received a missing-person report from one source and a juvenile runaway from another. The second mentioned you may have taken two hundred dollars."

Silence.

"Well?"

"Yes," I said. "I did."

"Son," said McDevitt, "what were you doing?"

"Nothing."

"Nothing," he said flatly.

I took a deep breath. "Leaving."

"Leaving? With a baby?" The man shook his head. "How far did you think you could go?"

Wyoming. New York City.

I kept my mouth shut. The pancakes and peanut butter, the yellow room, the pictures of happy animals—everything I had planned for Grover was disappearing in the glare of these questions.

The policeman behind the wheel interrupted. "Let's bring them in," he said, "before we float away in this rain."

At the police station McDevitt parked us in a wooden chair in the corner and brought me a roll of brown paper towels. I ripped off a few and tried to blot Grover dry. Everything around me was blurry: the too bright lights, the smell of wet cloth and coffee, Grover's screams when they tried to part us. McDevitt gave me a blue pen to, he said, "write down exactly what happened, in your own words." That no-good pen. The ink bled into my hand, blobbing the *e* and *o* when I signed and dated my story. Then McDevitt brought us two doughnuts. Powdered sugar. Grover was white as a snowman in three seconds flat. And Lambie Pie looked like a scrawny snow sheep.

McDevitt stayed close. Was he afraid I'd suddenly jump up? Grab Grover? Run? He didn't have to worry. I was so tired I could barely sit straight. The man offered me a

Coke but I waved it away. "Grover will want some," I explained. "The caffeine will give him the jitters."

"He doesn't need any help in that department," McDevitt said since, of course, Grover was howling, loud and long, for the Coke. "Does he always make this much noise?"

"He's tired," I defended the kid. "Do you have any milk?"

"How about an orange soda?"

And soon Grover was sporting an orange moustache and had learned a new word: *sodie*.

That's when Tracey arrived.

"Where's Grover?" I heard her voice. "Where in God's name is my baby?"

Chapter Twenty-three

I hunched in my seat and pulled Grover close. My heart speeded up.

"Easy, Ms. Graham," McDevitt soothed. "We've got both boys right here."

I saw Tracey enter the room and suddenly stop. And her eyes—the blue gone to black, all pupil—stared straight at us. At me and her baby, hunched in the chair. Only she didn't take me in, I could tell. Just Grover.

"Ma-ma," he cried.

Then Tracey did something strange. Without turning away, still staring, she started to cry. The tears, black from her eye goop, slipped out her eyes and down her cheeks and into her trembling mouth, and she didn't wipe them or turn away or stop.

Jenny came up behind Tracey, crossed the room, and took Grover from me. Her face was white and set.

"Sodie!" Grover grabbed for the can in my fist.

I let it go and, of course, the orange drink slopped out of

the can and onto the floor. But even aware of the spreading puddle, I could only sit, watching Tracey.

Jenny kissed Grover's hair, his cheek.

"Sodie!" the little guy crowed, waving his empty can.

"Tracey left him alone." I gripped Lambie Pie. Glanced down at the powdered sugar on my shorts.

Jenny bounced Grover gently in her arms but her voice was cold. "And that gave you the right to take him?"

"Anyone could have," I said.

Jenny was watching her sister. "Tracey called me at work and her voice was so . . . I don't know how to describe it. I dropped everything. We searched the building," she said softly, "the Dumpster."

So Tracey had been scared, really scared, I thought. Good.

"We even searched the street. Tracey thought . . . she thought Grover might have been hit by a car."

"He could have been," I said, aiming my words, small and hard, at Tracey.

"It happened so fast. How could it happen so fast?" Jenny seemed to be talking more to herself than to me. She continued to bounce Grover. "Tracey ran upstairs to get a few toys and then the phone rang and . . ." Jenny shifted Grover to her hip. "What I don't understand, Ben, is why, when you saw Grover alone . . . ? Why didn't you just stay with him till Tracey came back?"

If you helped Tracey—I remembered Mrs. T.'s question at that stupid picnic—*don't you think you'd be helping Grover, too?*

I blanked out the words. "She left him alone," I said loudly.

"Yes, she did"—Jenny's voice was bleak—"and you took him—"

"She left him alone," I repeated.

"And both of you"—Jenny spoke over me—"both of you could have hurt Grover."

Not me, I thought fiercely. I was trying to save him.

"La!" Grover cried.

I handed him Lambic Pie and watched as Jenny carried the kid and his toy to her sister. When Tracey clutched them, powdered sugar went all over her T-shirt. Even then she didn't stop crying.

Grover peered into her face, touched her cheek. "Wet, wet," he murmured as they followed McDevitt out the door.

I heard their voices, heard the words "kidnap" and "press charges," and then I didn't hear anything more.

She left him alone. I held tight to those words. I was right to do what I did.

It was strange how Tracey had cried without hardly making a sound.

I blanked out my sudden mind-picture of Tracey. Her face all quivery. Her black, quiet tears.

She left him alone. She left him alone. She left him alone.

When McDevitt returned, I said the words right out loud. "She left him alone. I wrote the whole thing down. What are you going to do?"

McDevitt ran a hand over his face. "She left her child

alone," he said tiredly. "I can't tell you how many parents do that. It was just for a minute, they tell me. After the accident."

"Then Tracey shouldn't have Grover, right?" I asked.

"Leaving her kid alone was stupid—and possibly dangerous." McDevitt tossed me a few paper towels and bent to wipe up the orange soda. "I bet she won't do it again. You saw the poor girl. She couldn't stop crying."

McDevitt straightened. "But I'm also wondering about you. When you saw that kid alone, why didn't you return him to his mother? Or just sit with him till she came back? Or even call the police?"

I kept my mouth shut.

McDevitt took the soggy towels from me. "I don't know much about you, Ben, but I know a little about people. Were you trying to protect the kid?" He glanced at me sharply. "Or get back at the mother?"

Both of you could have hurt Grover. Jenny's words ran through my head.

The towels dripped on McDevitt's shiny shoes. The man sighed. "Sit down, Ben," he said. "I'll get you a Coke."

I was still sitting there, Coke can unopened, when Mr. T. arrived.

Everything pulsed under those harsh lights. They played tricks with Mr. T.'s face. Left his cheeks sagging, his eyes peering from folds of skin. I had to glance away.

"Ahhh," the man said.

"A theft of two hundred dollars—and you don't want to press charges?" McDevitt asked behind him.

Mr. T. shook his head. "I want to take Ben home."

"You're able to, um, watch him closely?" McDevitt hesitated. "After all, he ran away. He abducted a child."

Mr. T. rubbed the space between his eyes. "Yes," he said.

The glaring lights seemed to tick.

Mr. T. and McDevitt spoke in low voices; then Mr. T. signed some papers and turned. I followed him out the door. I suppose I should have said "thank you" or "goodbye" to McDevitt, but, I don't know, those lights seemed to have zapped all my thoughts.

Mr. T. opened the car door—the one with the broken lock—for me. *Shlip-shlip* went the windshield wipers as he drove. The rain still slashed down, at the same pace, the same angle. That was strange. Surely days had passed since I first saw the step, step, step of those shiny black shoes. Since I had watched the silver bus pull away. Since I had followed McDevitt to the squad car.

"We'll spend the night at a motel," Mr. T. said, pulling into a drive and parking beside a pink neon sign. "I don't trust myself to keep driving."

The first words he had spoken to me since "Ahhh."

Mr. T. checked us into the Montgomery Motel and lead me to a blue door the same as every other blue door in the long row of blue doors.

Part of my brain still seemed to be stuck. In the motel room I could see two beds covered with blue spreads, a painting of a sailboat on the tan wall, one skinny chair— but they didn't seem real. I unwrapped a teeny soap and washed my face and hands. I watched the dirty suds

147

swirl down the drain. Watched the clean water run for a while.

When I came out of the bathroom, Mr. T. was hunched in the chair. His cap was still on his head, his big hands on his knees. He looked like Papa Bear in Baby Bear's chair.

He glanced at me, then glanced away.

I crawled into bed and listened to Mr. T. get ready. I shut my eyes. On my closed lids I kept seeing pictures: Grover alone in the dirt. Tracey's black tears. Mr. T. hunched in that spindly chair.

I woke up suddenly. The pink neon glowed, like a weird night-light, through the curtains. It dimly lit the next bed and Mr. T.'s sleeping back, and settled on the shorts I had slung on a chair.

Carefully, I slipped out of bed and dug into my four pockets. I drew out the bills—$153—and tucked them on the bureau beside Mr. T.'s keys.

Mr. T. snuffled once as I crept back. I froze, not wanting to wake him. That's when I noticed the pink light shifting over my bedside table, over a cup of water and a sandwich in a plastic bag. Crunchy peanut butter. Jif. I could tell from the first bite. I sipped the water, ate half the sandwich.

I thought of Mr. T. putting the snack on the table while I slept. *A little pick-me-up,* Gram would have said. I thought of Mr. T.'s hand on my shoulder in the hardware store and the warm smell of Gram's Ben-gay. I thought of Grover, all sticky, snoozing against me on the bus. The cut feeling came back to my insides again, but I finally fell asleep.

The next morning on the way back to Greenfield, Mr. T. once asked why and how, but "I don't know" was all I replied. I wasn't being sarcastic. It's just that everything was jumbled.

A, B, C rattled in my brain.

No sooner had Mr. T. parked the Torglemobile than Kate and Lenora were out the door. Lenora waved her Barbie, still wearing the rubber-band shoes I had made. Kate asked, "Are you going to jail?"

Chapter Twenty-four

Blank. Blank. Blank.

B I willed myself to continue floating in sleep. Unawake. Unaware. I squeezed my eyes against morning; the light pushed at my lids. I tried to shut out birdsong, the clatter of dishes. But to shut them out completely meant I'd have to close the bedroom door and window, which meant I'd have to push myself up from the too soft mattress, feel the wood floor under my feet, feel Charmaine's nubbly rug, walk. I'd have to be awake. Aware.

I opened one eye, then the other. The trophy guys stared back at me; the little flashlight gleamed. The curtains stirred at the window. I could feel sweat on my back, the heat weighing me down. Everything was the same as before Mr. T. and I went to town.

The last two days could have been a dream.

But they weren't.

The clock on the table said 9:05. I got out of bed and dressed, then pulled my suitcase out of the closet, smoothed the brown vinyl, quickly unlocked the second pocket. I counted out one ten-dollar bill, six fives and seven ones: $47. Exactly what I had paid for the bus tickets and supplies for Grover, minus the nineteen cents in change that had been mine. Here was the money I still owed Mr. T.

I slipped it on top of the cluttered desk in the Torgles' empty bedroom. I was going to write a note but I couldn't think of any words.

Blank. I blanked out all thought of packing my suitcase. I knew I'd have to do it soon. I was temporary. Besides, after what had happened, why would the Torgles want me to stay?

As I slipped down the stairs I heard Mr. T.'s mumble from the dining room, then Mrs. T.'s voice, tired and without any tone. "I still don't understand why Ben didn't return Grover to Tracey. Or call us."

I froze on the bottom stair.

"What if the baby had gotten sick?" asked Mrs. T. "What would Ben have done?"

Both of you could have hurt Grover, Jenny had said.

Not me, I wanted to cry. Never. Never.

"Stealing, kidnapping," Mrs. T. continued. "Of course, Ben will never be able to visit Grover. Tracey won't allow it. He's lucky Jenny talked her out of pressing charges."

I turned quickly and retraced my steps. Tracey was free to hurt me any way she could. Let her press charges. Let her damage my record. I didn't want to be grateful to her.

Were you trying to protect the kid? Or get back at the mother? I blanked out McDevitt's words as I sat on Jake's bed. I focused hard on my rules. *Blend in. Keep cash in a safe place. Keep secrets to yourself. Keep holding on to that*

151

mind-picture of you at eighteen, leaving the system. Walking away from it all.

I'd let myself get mushy, that was the problem. Kissy-kissy. Huggy-huggy. If you care in the system, you're a goner. Leave me alone, that's all I ask.

From the open window came the jibber-jabber of the twins. I bet they were playing their usual silly game of princess under the sweetgum tree.

I heard "Bang" and "Aargh" and then Kate said, "You're under arrest, Ben."

The twins were acting out what had happened to me.

Cop Barbie and Outlaw Barbie. Guns, shooting, blood, handcuffs.

I wanted to yell at them. I wanted to tell them they had the story all wrong.

Instead I continued to sit. I'd rather go to the juvenile home than stay here any longer, I decided. I'd rather go back to sorry Saint Stephen's. If the Torgles thought I'd stick around, weeping and wailing and waiting for the boot, they had another thought coming.

I'll call Ms. Burkell. I'll pack my suitcase right now.

Thump . . . thump. Mr. T.'s Frankenstein footsteps stopped outside my door. "Ben, do you want any breakfast?"

When I didn't answer, I heard him *thump . . . thump* away.

After a while, I got up and turned all the trophy guys to face the wall. All those eyes—it was too much. I didn't want anyone staring at me. I wished I could just blend into the brown-plaid bedspread.

I heard another set of footsteps. A rap at the door.

"Ben, may I come in?"

My social worker.

She *would* have to come nosing around. And I knew Ms. Burkell wouldn't leave till she had Ben-ed me at least a hundred times and clicked her beads a hundred more. I might as well get her yak-yak over with, I figured, opening the door. I'd just blank out everything she said.

Of course she opened with a question—"May I sit down?"—and waited till I gave a teeny nod before settling into a chair. She rested her hands on the notebook in her lap.

Ms. Burkell asked me to tell her what had happened, and I gave her the facts. It didn't take very long.

She leaned forward. "And now you want to go to Saint Stephen's?"

"Yes."

"Ben." I could tell she was working up to some meaningful contact. Her beads trembled. "Is that what you *really* want?"

What I *really* wanted. What *did* I really want? Well, it sure wasn't this. Chaos with a capital *C*. Two motormouth girls. An old Frankenstein and his flea wife and their needy-greedy mutt. A baby who wasn't even there.

I didn't want anyone giving me flashlights or eating my pancakes or reaching up to hold my hand. I didn't want anyone hollering, all happy, "Beh! Beh! Beh!"

I crossed my arms tightly. My heart felt ready to bust with all I didn't want.

And another thing I didn't want. I didn't want anyone to ask me what I really wanted. Like it mattered. Like it would make a difference. And I didn't want any more questions—not one more—from this woman. This woman with her talk of fairy god-awful mothers. With her stupid-looking hair.

All those *didn't wants* built and built in my chest.

I opened my mouth. "I hate your beads!" I yelled.

Chapter Twenty-five

Ms. Burkell blinked. She touched one of her hair beads. She glanced down at her notebook like it held the right things to say. Her face was still in meaningful-contact mode but her lips twitched.

"So, what you want—let me get this straight—what you *really* want is for me to remove my beads?"

Why was she smiling? Didn't she realize she'd just been insulted?

I looked away. I didn't care what she did with her dumb beads. Leave me alone, that's all I ask.

And that's what I told her I wanted.

When Ms. Burkell left, taking her notebook and her cheery beads, I went back to sitting on Jake's bed. Why did she have to come? If I was down before, now I felt lower than the floor. What did Ms. Burkell know about wanting? Wanting was like blabbing and boo-hooing. Never changed a thing. It just busted you up inside.

I tried to blank out all my *didn't want*s before they could mess with me again. I bent my mind to some plans. School would be starting in about two weeks. And I'd be leaving soon for Saint Stephen's. I should start blanking out both Torgles now. Right this minute. Blank. Blank. And the twins. Kate. Blank. Lenora. Blank.

I tried to hold on to that mind-picture of me at eighteen, walking away from Greenfield. Walking away from it all.

The next day I stayed in Jake's room as much as I could. Mrs. T. wouldn't let the twins tease me out. "Ben needs his privacy," I heard her explain outside my closed door.

"But I have to show him the Roman dress I fixed for my Barbie," Lenora said, adding loudly: "It goes with the shoes he made."

Toga, I wanted to explain, though I kept my mouth shut. A Roman dress is a toga.

"Ben's busy, dear."

"Doing what?" asked Kate.

"He's packing, isn't he?" asked Lenora. "I heard you talking to that lady with the beads."

"We don't know—" began Mrs. T.

"Packing?" Kate cried. "Why?"

"He's leaving," Lenora said flatly. "Everyone does."

Yeah, kids, I thought. Welcome to the system.

Strays. We were all strays. Actually, we were lower than strays. We were gumballs. No-good-to-anyone gumballs. Plopping down at one home or another. Stepped on and kicked and carted away.

Riding high on that Greyhound bus, I had thought Grover and I had shaken the system. Right. Our escape had been pitiful. And I hadn't helped Grover at all. He was right back with Tracey.

Well, boo-hooing wasn't going to help. I gave myself a shake and jumped off that plaid bedspread. If I was leaving for Saint Stephen's in a day or two, I might as well clean Jake's room now. Get it ready for the next gumball kid to plop down.

I got out my suitcase and counted my money. I wanted to make sure the count was accurate before I brought my hard-earned cash anywhere near those light-fingered Saint Stephen's boys. Then I checked under the bed. A few dust bunnies, one sock, and two books: *Where Eagles Dare* and Dr. Spock's *Baby and Child Care*. The first was weeks overdue and the second . . . well, I almost tossed it. But twenty-five cents was twenty-five cents. I decided to resell it to the library.

I could hear Kate and Lenora tiptoeing up and down the hall. There were a few whispers and a rustle. A piece of paper slid under the door.

I let it lie for a minute; then I picked it up.

At first that note made no sense at all. The page was covered with big, loopy writing and more exclamation marks than a houseful of shouts. Each letter was a different color. That page looked like some fool rainbow had spilled over it.

> Dear Ben!!
> BON VOYAGE!!!!!
>
> xoxox,
> Lenora and Kate
>
> P.S. We miss you! Don't go!!!!!

I read the note again. I pictured the girls choosing each crayon. Fighting over whose name should go first. *Lenora and Kate*. Well, it was clear who had won that fight. Maybe the old Barbie-biting Jango had ditched both her nickname and her place as Kate's shadow.

Bon voyage. The girls must have remembered the message on Grover's party balloon. *We miss you.* That busted-chest feeling was back. I tried to blank it out. I'd never thought of being missed when I moved on. Of someone feeling sad. Sure, I'd gotten a good-bye present from Myron the Chihuahua, but that was just Mrs. DeBernard acting cute.

I folded the note and tucked it carefully into its very own pocket in my suitcase. It might be nice to have at Saint Stephen's.

Over the next few days, I tried to call Ms. Burkell but ended up leaving messages on her answering machine. Why was my move taking so long? Saint Stephen's was bound to have an opening. After all, foster families might be scarce, but the juvenile home could always cram a kid in.

Finally Ms. Burkell called. My paperwork was completed. I'd be moved in two days.

Good, I told myself as I listened. Good, I repeated as I passed the phone to Mr. T. at Ms. Burkell's request. Good. Good. Good. I marched up the stairs and into Jake's room and started packing.

And in less than ten minutes, here came Mr. T.'s *thump . . . thump.* He insisted I come to town with him. Wouldn't take no for an answer.

As he drove I gave him a side-eyes glance. What could he want? He didn't say a word. The only sound was the hot wind whipping through windows, the usual rattles, the jiggling door.

I remembered his silence after he picked me up from the police station.

He was going to get me alone and give me the boot. *Bye, Ben. The summer was nice. Here's our address. Keep in touch.* I'd heard it all before.

Well, I planned to say good-bye first.

Digging into my pocket, I closed a fist around my money. I had chosen the twenty-dollar bill from the second pocket of my suitcase. If we stopped for lunch, I wanted to pay my own way. I'd *insist* on paying, to use Mr. T.'s words. I didn't want to take anything more from him.

We made the rounds. The hardware store, with not one customer inside. Safeway. I didn't feel like going to the library, so we passed by.

Then Mr. T. stopped at Uddleston's. No big deal, right? A cheap treat for the foster kid.

Except Uddleston's was right next to the Greyhound station.

I knew why Mr. T. had insisted I come. To remind me of all the trouble I'd caused. What better place to give me the boot?

We entered Uddleston's, chose red stools at the counter. Mr. T. ordered two milk shakes.

"Ahhh," he said when they arrived. He poked a straw into his cup. "Nothing better than a cold shake"—he slurped—"on a hot summer day."

I watched a silver bus pull up. That feeling was building in my chest again. I tried to blank it out. I'd do it again, I thought fiercely. I'd steal the money, the kid. I'd run.

You . . . could have hurt Grover, Jenny had said.

Suddenly I put my head on the counter. My chest was heaving. It was busting for sure. I cried, and under my folded arms the tears made a little pool. I heard the *chuggety-chug* of the milk shake machine.

Then I felt Mr. T.'s big hand on my back. Pat-pat-pat.

I tried to shrug it off, but the patting continued. Slow, steady. I didn't want the man treating me like a baby. Ben Watson could take care of himself.

I tried to stop but the tears just came worse. All Tracey's crying in the police station—had she felt this way, too, when she thought Grover was gone?

I thought of the kid's almighty big grin on the whirl-go-round. The way he squeezed Lambie Pie when he was scared. How he shared his Cheese Nip with me.

Pat-pat-pat.

I cried for a long time. When I finally stopped, the counter under my cheek was warm and wet.

Mr. T. pushed a napkin close to my hand. Without raising my head, I squished it over my nose and blew.

The man continued to pat, then started talking in that slow way of his. "I did love the way Grover ate," he said. "Happy to have the food outside and in." Mr. T. chuckled. "Remember the time he plopped mashed potatoes on top of his head?"

Those potatoes had looked like a lumpy cap. White, lumpy cap on his Tweety Bird head.

"What did you like?" asked Mr. T.

I didn't want to talk. I didn't want the tears to come back.

Finally I whispered from the cave of my crossed arms, "I liked how he said 'Beh.' "

"Ahhh," said Mr. T. "He said 'Beh' a lot. Grover sure singled you out."

I blinked back tears. To the kid I'd been more than a camouflage fish. More than someone just blending in.

Mr. T. and I sat quiet as the counter dried and the tightness eased in my throat. I raised my head, blew my nose again.

Mr. T. was gazing at a silver bus through the window. "Your social worker says you want to leave." He fiddled with his straw. "She said you want to go to that juvenile home."

I fiddled with my straw, too.

"I know things are different with Grover gone," Mr. T. continued. "But won't you stay with us at least till the social worker gets you a new family?"

"No," I said quickly. I wanted to leave. Now.

We watched as folks slowly boarded the bus. I saw one woman wave to another.

Mr. T. suddenly spoke. "Hello. Good-bye. Remember how Grover's wave used to stand for both words?"

I nodded.

"Sometimes a person's good-bye can be a big wish for hello."

Were we still talking about Grover? I wasn't sure.

"Maybe," Mr. T. continued, "a person has heard good-bye so many times the word just jumps out of his mouth. Maybe it is the first thing he thinks to say."

I puzzled over Mr. T.'s words. They were as confusing as his talk about taking and giving that day we fixed the torn card. As confusing as that stuff about people destroying what they wanted most. The man better watch it. He was starting to sound like Ms. Burkell.

Mr. T. smiled. "Just think about it," he said. "Now, would you like to split a sandwich or something?"

After we had eaten, I tried to pay my share but Mr. T. closed my fingers over the twenty-dollar bill.

I didn't even fight him. I tried to dig up that old feeling, that feeling of refusing to take. But somehow—it was strange—all that crying must have rearranged my insides. I couldn't make the hardness come back.

We settled into our usual quiet as Mr. T. drove, heading not home, but out on Route 3. When he stopped at the new shopping center, I could see why this place was taking the business from Greenfield. The shops downtown were tiny and old compared to these gleaming stores.

When Mr. T. had parked, he sat, hands on the steering wheel, checking out that hardware store. It stretched out, all shiny clean, with lumber stacked neatly outside. "Why don't you check out the toy store," he said, not turning his head, "while I pick up a part for the mower?"

"Why don't you buy it—," I began, then cut myself off. Most likely Mr. T.'s dusty store didn't carry the part.

Staring at this nuts-and-bolts mansion, I realized—and maybe Mr. T. did, too—that the old store downtown wouldn't last long. Sooner or later Mr. T. would have to move on.

"Thirty-eight years," he said.

Jeesh, the man had been working at that poor hole since way before I was born. He'd never had Job Number Two or Five or Seven. He'd been at Number One all this time.

It must be hard for him to blank out and move on. I

thought about patting his back—but didn't. Instead I borrowed some of Mrs. T.'s tone. "A part for the mower," I said. "You mean something's going to get fixed?"

My joke worked. Mr. T.'s face lightened. "Now, don't you start," he said, shooing me out the car door. "Bad enough there's Eileen."

I headed to a huge toy store. The doors parted, just like Safeway's, and then the noise hit. Whirring, beeping, buzzing, popping. And kid squeals like Kate at her loudest. I'd never seen so many toys crammed into one place. Video games, action figures, stuffed bears, cars. And Barbies. Stacks and stacks of Barbies. Pink Ice Barbie, Hula Hair Barbie, Cool Shopping Barbie. The shelves gave off a glow like a UFO.

Maybe I'd get a present for the twins. A good-bye present. I remembered the yellow Lambie Pie ribbon they'd given Grover. They might like something fancy for their dolls.

I checked out the shelves. Barbie clothes, skis, shoes, phones, and cars were stacked in pink boxes clear to the ceiling. I grabbed a box with a long gold dress, long gold gloves, and teeny gold sandals. The whole getup glittered like the crown of a princess. Kate would love it.

Shopping for Lenora's Barbie took more time. Those chewed-on feet were a challenge. But after thumbing through about a thousand boxes, I found one called Swinging in the Rain. It held a yellow slicker, umbrella, and best of all, high yellow boots. This footgear sure beat those rubber-band shoes I had made. Now no one would know that Lenora's pitiful Barbie once had doubled as a thumb.

After paying, I still had some time, so I decided to check out the little-kid toys. Talk about pint-sized. The play rakes were hardly bigger than forks. I touched a green bucket with a grinning sea horse. I'd had one like it at my Number Two.

Suddenly a banshee yell came from the next aisle, followed by "Po! Po! Po!"

And then I heard "No. Give it to Mama."

Grover.

And Tracey.

Chapter Twenty-six

I scooched to the edge of the aisle and peered around the corner.

"Po! Po!" Grover clutched a toy phone. He shook his head so fiercely his yellow curls bobbed.

"Please, Grover," said Tracey.

Still shaking his head, the kid skedaddled down the aisle. Tracey followed, clutching Lambie Pie. She swiped at the phone. Grover speeded up, turned.

Saw me.

"Beh! Beh! Beh!"

He came at me full tilt. Nose-dived into my knee—*whack!*—with the force of Charmaine's wagging tail.

"Hey, big guy." I palmed his head.

"You." The word slapped me. Frowning, Tracey strode up the aisle.

"Po! Po!"

"I suppose you were spying on me." Tracey tried to

loosen Grover's grasp on my leg. "Sneaking around. Trying to find out what I'm doing wrong."

"Po!" screamed Grover.

As fast as Tracey lifted the fat little fingers, they'd clamp down again. The octopus grip.

I waited for the old anger at Tracey to hit me. It wasn't there.

Instead I felt almost sorry for her. Her face was as red as Grover's. As the kid shrieked people turned to stare. Shoot, I knew what she was going through. Grover had screeched "keam" in the same piercing way.

"Want me to try?" I asked, hunkering down. I held my fist to my ear. "Brring. Brrring."

Grover closed his mouth, blue eyes on me.

"Hello. Hello." I nodded, listening to my fist. "What? You want to speak to Grover?"

The kid's eyes lit up.

"Wait, I'll see if he's here." I held my fist out to Grover. "Call for you, big guy."

Grover brought my fist to his ear. "Hel-wo." The toy phone dropped. Tracey pounced on it, placing it high on a shelf.

"Hello, Grover." I put on a deep voice. "This is Mr. T."

"Tee!" cried Grover. He blinked, waiting for more. His whole body trembled with excitement.

"Um," I said.

Tracey stroked Grover's head. "You're stuck now," she told me, but it didn't sound mean.

Then Grover brought my fist close to his chest. "Beh!" he cried, hugging it.

His shirt was apple-juice damp and sticky, but I let the

hug go on. "Yeah, okay," I mumbled. "It's nice to see you, too."

Tracey crossed her arms, squishing Lambie Pie. The pitiful toy was now missing an eye. "You could have hurt him, you know," she said suddenly. "Where would he have slept? What about food?"

I thought of the yellow room and animal stencils and meals full of pancakes and Jif. A dream I knew I couldn't make real.

Tracey smoothed Lambie Pie's ribbon. "Food, rent—I think about them all the time. Insurance, clothes, new shoes. Sometimes I wake up at night—"

"You left him alone," I broke in. "You hurt him, too."

"Yeah." Tracey's face closed over. "I made a mistake, a big one." She reached for Grover. "Time to go, baby."

Rrriiipp.

"Oh, Grover. No."

"Po," he said defiantly.

That fast, he had grabbed and opened a box. He hauled out the plastic horse inside.

Tracey reached for the toy. "Honey," she said, "we can't afford—"

"Neigh, neigh." Grover galloped the horse through the air.

I thought of my horse salt and pepper shakers at Gram's. "Let me buy it for him," I said.

Tracey's jaw tensed. "I don't take handouts."

"Neither do I."

The girl tried to stare me down, but I stared right back.

"I still won't let you see him," she said.

"I know," I answered. "I just want to buy him a present."

When I got back to the Torglemobile, my twenty-dollar bill was down to a few pennies and dimes. Mr. T. pointed to my bag. Something for the twins, I explained. I didn't say anything about Grover, the toy horse, and Tracey. I wanted to puzzle that out myself.

Tracey hadn't wanted to take that toy horse from me. But she did. For Grover. Mrs. T. had said we competed over Grover. I remembered how I'd tried to keep Tracey away. I liked it when Grover pushed her aside and reached for me. Maybe I was jealous. Maybe I had taken Grover that day because I wanted to get back at her. I wanted to protect the kid, yes, but I also wanted to hurt Tracey. Show her what a lousy mother she was. Prove she should never have left him.

I remembered riding high with Grover on that Greyhound bus, escaping Greenfield just like my mother. Only she had left me behind.

Chapter Twenty-seven

That evening I asked Mr. T.'s permission to use the phone in their bedroom. I said there were two calls I needed to make. In *private*, I added, with a glance at the twins.

Of course Charmaine had to follow me and lie panting at my feet. "Okay," I said, "but don't blame me if you hear yelling from the other end."

I picked up the black phone and quickly punched in the number. As soon as a voice answered, I said the words before I could chicken out: "I'm sorry."

"Who is this?"

"Ben Watson." I took a deep breath. "I'm sorry."

Silence on the other end, then: "I don't want you to call."

"I just wanted to say what I did."

"And that's supposed to make everything all right?"

"I didn't think—"

"You still can't see Grover."

"I know," I said. "That's not why I called."

More silence, then *click . . . click . . . click*. I pictured a blue-moon fingernail tapping the phone.

"Jenny says maybe I'm being too hard."

Stubborn can make you tough or hard, I remembered Jenny saying. I had been hard, too.

Tracey continued, "And Eileen Torgle told me you've been knocked around a lot."

I was surprised. "That's what Mrs. T. says about you."

"Ha." Tracey's bark of a laugh. "Everyone's a shrink."

Click . . . click . . . click.

"You going to steal Grover again?"

"Not unless you leave him alone."

A long pause. I waited for Tracey to hang up, but instead she said something so low I had to strain to catch it. "We both did something we won't do again," she said. "Let's leave it at that."

I could hear "Po! Po! Po!" in the background.

After hanging up, I rested my head on the wall. "One call down," I said to Charmaine, who thumped her tail. The dog was like my own private cheerleader. Even without yelling, the next call was going to be hard.

I hated to lay out my plans and not follow through. I hated not wanting to say good-bye. That busted-chest feeling was back. Shoot, I hated that, too.

I dialed superfast and, when I heard "hello," rushed out all my words.

No sooner had I finished than Ms. Burkell started talking. I pictured the bounce-bounce-bounce of her beads. She said she would deal with the paperwork immediately. Then she asked what the Torgles had said.

I swallowed. "They don't know."

"You mean they haven't asked you to stay past the summer?" Ms. Burkell sounded surprised, then her voice softened. "Ben, this arrangement was just temporary, you know. I've heard the hardware store could close any day now. What if the Torgles can't take you for more than an extra month or so?"

"Then that's all the time I have."

"Okay," she said finally. "At least you can ask, right? Meanwhile, I'll keep looking for something more permanent."

I wanted to tell her not to bother—I was used to impermanent—but I knew she was just doing her job. Besides, there was something else I wanted to say.

"Um," I began, "about your beads."

"The ones you hate."

"I don't *hate* them," I said.

Ms. Burkell laughed. "Ben, when I ask you a question— any question—your answer is usually 'nothing.' I was glad to hear you say anything else."

"So you're not insulted?"

Ms. Burkell laughed again. "You should hear what my mother says."

That night in Jake's room I tried to work out the asking-to-stay scene with the Torgles in my mind. I tried it A, B, C. Then I tried it B, Z, Q. I had the trophy guys act out different parts. I must have worked that scene a hundred possible ways. Who would say what when. How the Torgles would look if they said yes. What I would do if they said no.

The reality was chaos with a capital *C*.

I'd decided to talk to the Torgles at breakfast. Except

Kate and Lenora were fighting over how to spend their dad's forty dollars. Charmaine was woofing at a speck on the floor. And Mrs. T. was leveling some tone at her husband because the screen door *still* wasn't fixed.

I must have tried to break in a hundred times: "I wonder if you . . ." "How about if . . ." "What would you say . . ."

Finally I took a deep breath. "I want to stay past the summer," I practically hollered. "If that's okay with you."

Then it was chaos with all capital letters: *C-H-A-O-S*. Underlined. In fact, only one person said the words I'd imagined. Mrs. T. kept repeating, "Okay? *Okay?*" The twins jabbered and leaped. Charmaine barked like a crazy dog. But Mr. T., with his hands on his knees, winked and made the very sound I'd hoped for. He said, "Ahhh."

Chapter Twenty-eight

October. It's been two months since I made those two phone calls.

Mr. T. and I are off this afternoon to downtown Greenfield. Of course, the twins are as jealous green as two grassy lawns, but Mrs. T. sweet-talked their sulks away by promising to help make new Barbie clothes.

"It's not fair," Kate grumbled at breakfast.

"Ben always gets to see them," whined Lenora.

"Not *always*." Mrs. T. smiled at me. "In fact, this is the very first time."

Hopefully it won't be the last.

Mr. T. hums as he drives. The trees along the road are now sporting colored leaves. October is the one month when Greenfield might become Goldfield, say, or Redfield. And the sweetgum tree in the Torgles' yard is now fancy as a party. Its five-pointed leaves have turned all different shades: yellow, dark purple, and red. Today that pitiful thing looks like a bouquet of stars.

The trees we're passing get me thinking about the family tree, that stupid school assignment that's due on Monday. My tree, all bare but for three named twigs. Well, at least I won't have to stay up all night trying to finish it.

October. The twins are starting to talk Halloween. Or maybe I should say yell Halloween. Kate wants them to dress as princesses; Lenora refuses. They argue about how to spend the last few dimes of their father's money. Blabbing and boo-hooing, they constantly barge into my room.

It is chaos with a capital *C*.

Mrs. T. is fast-forwarding to Christmas, when Saint Jake Jock will visit. I wonder how he'll feel about a stranger in his room. One day I had returned from school to find the twelve trophy guys gone. When I asked, Mrs. T. replied, "It was time I put them away. This is *your* room now."

I have started to put a few things—my things—on the shelves. To keep my flashlight company. Mrs. T. keeps asking if I would like a new bedspread, but I am used to that brown plaid. A new spread might give me the feeling I've moved again. And I plan to stay at Number Eight for a while, thank you very much.

As the Torglemobile rattles down the highway, I try to keep my thoughts from jumping ahead to this afternoon. I let them bounce: D. M. Z. Q.

"We'll go to your hardware store first," I say. "Then the library and Safeway."

"Aye, aye, sir." Mr. T. salutes.

I settle back, glad the hardware store has managed to

hang on this long. I want it to be part of today. This day I have planned so carefully: A, B, C.

We'll finish at Uddleston's. Vanilla shakes and red straws for the three of us. Mr. T., Grover, and me.

See, about two weeks after that first phone call, Kate came giggling into the living room. "Phone for Ben. It's a girl."

When I picked up, I heard a familiar voice. "Don't get any ideas."

I gripped the phone. Tracey Graham.

"All day I've heard nothing but 'po, po, po.' I tried the toy phone. No luck. Jenny tried books. Grover threw them. Nothing, I mean *nothing*, will distract him."

Sure enough, "Po! Po! Po!" came from the background.

"We've run out of people to call," she said. "You want to talk to Grover?"

And then I heard "Beh! Beh! Beh!"

In the weeks since that call there have been others. These days Grover is so phone obsessed I talk to him a few times a week. Perhaps *talk* is not quite the right word, since Grover babbles in a language I'm still translating: *po, Beh, Ma-ma, La, Tee, Ah-den* (Aunt Jenny), and about a hundred others, from *neigh* (horse) to *oos* (shoes).

And once Grover finishes, do you think that poor phone gets a rest? Not a chance. Tracey has to talk to Mrs. T., or Mrs. T. to her, the twins jabber for their turn, Mr. T. aahs around the kitchen, Charmaine follows like the man's tail-thumping shadow.

It is chaos with all capital letters: *C-H-A-O-S.*

For example, the other day Jenny asked my advice about pancakes and then Tracey took the phone and grilled me about toys—trikes versus wagons. Suddenly, out of nowhere, she said, "You know, Grover named that outlet thing you gave him."

"The night-light?"

"He calls it Boo Beh," said Tracey.

Blue Ben. How about that.

I still worry sometimes about Grover. Yeah, I know his sheets and faucets are okay, but what if, say, his mother died? And his aunt? What would happen to him?

Those questions—well, they keep me awake some nights. If I can think them through, lay out the answers like a trail of stones, then hopefully Grover can't get lost. The thinking is hard, though. No sooner do I have one question figured out than another comes along.

I remember Gram's will and the friend she left me to. Maybe Tracey's will should name a bunch of folks that can watch over Grover. I would like to be one of them. If something happened to Tracey and Jenny, I would promise to stay around. After all, only the Watson half of me is footloose; the other is stick-it-out stubborn as Gram. And since I'm only eleven—not eighty-two—there's a good chance I won't be dying till I've seen him safely grown.

Gram. The strong branch on my family tree. Maybe I can be a sort of twig on Grover's.

I remember the question Mrs. T. asked when I first came. Did I think of Grover more than I thought of myself?

Now I can answer that question: Yes.

Me, myself, I. The life of Ben Watson. I don't want to think about that. I don't want to think about all the homes it took to find this one. All the spoiled Chihuahuas and time-out closets, all the light-fingered boys and Safeway samples I had to pass through to get here.

Ms. Burkell wants me to talk all this out. Those are her words—"talk it all out"—like my mind is a sponge to be squeezed clean and dry. Like all that happened can be washed down the sink. She has set up an appointment with a fancy counselor. I tell Ms. Burkell she is shrink enough for me. She laughs but says all this talking will be healing for me.

Healing, huh. She makes me sound like Grover with a boo-boo on his knee. Right now, I don't want to talk. It is enough to walk beside the twins to the school bus. To help Mrs. T. fix a meal. To set my own place at the table. It is enough to sit on the brown-plaid spread each night and gaze at the sky and watch the small lights breaking through. In the fall in Greenfield, the stars are very clear and close.

Ms. Burkell's beads don't get on my nerves half as bad these days, even though she keeps yammering about this new law. There's a big push, she says, to promote adoption, to keep foster stays short, to place kids in permanent homes.

I'll believe it when I see it.

Though Ms. Burkell hasn't brought up Sarah Jewel again, sometimes I wonder about my mother. Maybe she had been knocked around, too, like Tracey. In my mind Sarah Jewel is always a dark-haired teenager staring out a bus window. But really, now, she would be grown up. A woman fixing meals, driving a car, working. Maybe she would have other children. And my father? What about him? Someday I may try to find out.

Not now. My parents are twigs, broken off, blown away. I want to let them rest for a while.

Two days ago Tracey asked Mr. T. if he'd like to take Grover into town on Saturday afternoon. And she asked me if I'd like to go, too.

Tracey was letting me spend a day with Grover. How about that. *We both did something we won't do again,* she had said in August on the phone. *Let's leave it at that.* I guess that's what she was doing.

I haven't seen the kid since the day I bought him that little horse. I bet he's taller now. And he's probably running fast as a colt.

I think Tracey has decided that Grover needs some guys in his life. Guys to read him stories, to play horse and car, to shuffle beside him while he names every bug, stick, and leaf in his path.

An old guy like Mr. T.

A young guy like me.

Good thing I never sold that Dr. Spock book back to the library. It's bound to come in handy.

I wonder if Dr. Spock has anything to say about family trees.

I think about the tree I inked up in class. Maybe what I need is not one tree but a little forest. A bunch of trees together on the same piece of paper. There would be a tree for Lenora and Kate and their broken twig of a dad. And one for the Torgles. And one for Grover and Tracey and Jenny. And my tree, too. Mine and Gram's.

And maybe some of these trees would be mighty oaks and pretty maples. But a fair number, I bet, would be sweetgums. Yes. Because, as Mrs. Crawdich used to say, a sweetgum can surprise you.

But who wants to think about homework? My mind is filled with plans for this afternoon. And this is how I'd like things to start.

Today when Tracey opens the door to apartment 402, I will hand her a bag of Grover's favorite fish crackers. I will hand her a big jar of Jif for Jenny, who's studying for an exam. Then I want to give something to Tracey. I want to look straight at her. I want to look past the quick frown and gooped-up lashes and see her eyes, the same blue as Grover's. And I want to say "Thank you."

I think she will understand.

Of course, the afternoon may not start like this at all. It will probably be chaos with all capital letters: *C-H-A-O-S*. Underlined. And I will have to work the thank-you in when I can.

ABOUT THE AUTHOR

Mary Quattlebaum is the author of several books for young readers, including *Jackson Jones and the Puddle of Thorns,* which won the Marguerite de Angeli Prize and a *Parenting* Reading Magic Award; *The Magic Squad and the Dog of Great Potential,* winner of the Sugarman Award; and most recently, the picture book *Aunt CeeCee, Aunt Belle, and Mama's Surprise,* which *Publishers Weekly* praised as a tale "readers will be happy to hear . . . over and over."

Mary Quattlebaum grew up in rural Virginia, the oldest of seven children. Like Ben Watson, she often took care of rambunctious younger brothers and sisters. She earned a B.A. from the College of William and Mary and an M.A. from Georgetown University. She now writes frequently for *The Washington Post* and various magazines for children and adults and teaches creative writing in Washington, D.C., where she lives with her husband and daughter.